T0106136

The Forever Question

Goonocracy

TONIS F.V. KASVAND

iUniverse, Inc.
New York   Bloomington

The Forever Question
Goonocracy

iUniverse books may be ordered through booksellers or by contacting:

iUniverse
1663 Liberty Drive
Bloomington, IN 47403
www.iuniverse.com
1-800-Authors (1-800-288-4677)

ISBN: 978-1-4502-3494-8 (pbk)
ISBN: 978-1-4502-3495-5 (cloth)
ISBN: 978-1-4502-3496-2 (ebk)

Printed in the United States of America

iUniverse rev. date: 7/21/2010

To my father, Micker, and my lost water brother.

Carrots killed the dinosaurs.

If you would like to contact the author directly, send your message via e-mail to theforeverquestion@gmail.com

The Internet makes you stupid.

Chapter 0
Projectile Supremacy

Slicing through the clouds, a newborn baby happily glides downward as an umbilical cord flaps furiously through the rushing draft. Baby sees patterns, feels emptiness, but euphoria fills the infant's youthful insides as the baby sees something approach to nurture a lost soul. The ground and the baby face each other, ready to duel as they meet.

The ground wins.

*   *   *

"Find my baby!" demands the emotional queen. Servants, warriors, chambermaids, anyone within shouting distance are tacitly assigned to search. One caregiver stays with the queen, sewing the wounds from a joyous-turned-infamous event. As the flushed queen gazes forebodingly around the lavish courtroom, which normally is used for important kingdom decision-making, her servants, who are dressed in ceremoniously expensive birthing attire, frantically consult one another in hurried discussion.

The queen shouts her discontent of emotional and physical pain. The horrific scream echoes over and over again down the large blue-hued hallway that connects to the glamorously decorated courtroom.

The caregiver refuses to acknowledge the queen's pain and continues to care for the uncontrolled post-birth bleeding. While courtroom servants focus their attention on the large red bed covered in quilted silks and blood, they notice the queen does not want their consult. Her chin digs into her chest, and she is only aware of her own pain and predicament.

Among the onlookers, a frightened boy tightly grips his mother's arm. He wants to know why the adults are dashing around the courtroom to the point of trampling him. His mother guides him into a room next to the chaos. She sits him down on a padded crystal bench. The boy's face begins to relax as his mother carefully crosses her legs and sits comfortably on the polished gray floor in front of him. He knows a good story is about to be told.

She speaks. "In this kingdom, the great kingdom of Ovulum, the people choose their future leaders when babies are born. They believe a strong mother will bear a strong child. Therefore, the birth is watched closely for the signs. The standard measurement of great leadership is if the mother can push the baby out of her womb for distance."

The boy winces, even though the shock of this ritual confuses him.

His mother continues. "If the baby survives the big push and is pushed the maximum distance of the umbilical cord, then that baby, male or female, will be given the training to be a great leader. The mother also receives special privileges for the honor of bearing a great child."

"When I was born, was I strong?" the little boy asks.

His mother assures him with an honest smile, "You did fine. You have a place here at the royal palace." The boy begins to understand, but what he witnessed recently in the courtroom was much different. He tries to recall the recent past.

*　　*　　*

The queen has her legs propped up high so everyone in the court can see the great event. Her legs collapse back onto her bed. The queen knows that the baby is about to be released, but she stops the process and tries to squeeze the baby back in by tightening her legs. A drink is hastily snatched, she drinks it quickly, and then she bounces her bottom up and down by lifting her body with her arms and dropping. Nobody knows exactly what she is doing, but a few mothers suspect that she is priming her insides using gaseous fluids. The more pressure she can put into her system, the greater chance that the baby will pop forward faster. She drinks again and again. Her insides stretch, waiting to explode. Screams fill the great hall as she raises her legs. Everyone leans in, looking for the head to crown. The crowd jostles as the newborn mass shoots out at a tremendous speed; it's like watching a cannon fire. Afterbirth splatters everywhere as the heap flies into the air, snapping the life-support cord and merrily finding a window escape route. The crowd is in awe as it wipes away the queen's fluids from their faces. The court jester is close to the window. When he looks outside, he can see a trail of fluid and a small mass bouncing from rooftop to rooftop, down the great mountain, until the baby mass is out of sight. He quickly removes a parchment from his hat and a writing utensil from his chest pocket. Bouncing baby jokes are on his mind.

While many people from the royal court search for the baby, the queen demands to see legal representation. She orders everyone to leave the courtroom, including her guards. She clasps her stomach carefully, moving her hands, and gently rubs her belly through the bed cover. *A tiny mass of flesh, without the concept of power, politics, or even speech, has my future. I made it. I cannot go back. I conceived uncertainty and a gamble, which may bring a legacy or eternal loss. I—*

The opening of the main courtroom door interrupts her thoughts, as five legal representatives enter the courtroom. Large, stiff packages are tied to their backs, legs, shoulders, and arms. They flaunt their muscular, stalwart bodies at the queen as they haul their bureaucracy to her bedside. The group of men slowly unstraps each heavy package, which they stack on the floor for easy access and prolific presentation. The queen does not understand why legal advisors encumber themselves by transporting legal books, case-law reports, and personal autobiographies of their achievements to every conceivable corner of the kingdom. Her only positive experience with this profession is the visual enjoyment of their muscular physiques. Otherwise, the culture of legal representation always brings her misery and agony. In her mind, she calls them Legal Advisory Dinks, or LADs—an uncomplimentary acronym she never reveals to anyone but which gives the court community speculative entertainment during boring receptions.

When the last LAD stacks his packages, the LAD with the tallest stack speaks. "My queen, my name is Head Legal Lead of the Royal Order of the Legal Advisory Department of the Kingdom of Ovulum in the World of O, sub-servant to the gods Zeezan, Yrtol …"

The queen sighs at the pompous declaration of his status. So far, she's listened to over one hundred words, and the LAD is still narrating his position in the known universe. The queen turns her head, looking for her royal bedpan. She imagines the liquid-filled object floating upward and toward the LADs, then pouring her discontent on every scrap of paper that covers her floor. Those papers give life to legal advisors. Any soiled destruction to their precious documents would give them eternal grief. She thinks, *Grief can be good.* She gazes at the group and then focuses on the young LAD, whose physique is peeking through his unbuttoned shirt. *He must have been rushed and forgot to cover his upper chest—a pleasant mistake I am willing to forgive during a bath with him at my side …*

Silence breaks her fantasy as the LAD stops speaking. The LAD had finally completed his BLAH, an acronym known to legal representatives as Beginning Listing and Heraldry, and known to others as Boastfully Long Auditory Heap. The business

4

of discussing her situation commences. Because the queen ignored his presentation, she improvises control and starts pointing to each of the men. "You, I will call One. You, Two. You, Three. You, Four." The last unnamed LAD is the young man she dreams to share intimacy with at a more private moment. "What is your name?" she asks hungrily.

One, the only LAD who presented himself to the queen, notices his young counterpart's exposed chest. "Pilastama, fix your shirt!"

Hoping to distract and stop the young lad from complying with the order, the queen forcefully speaks. "I assume your legal team understands the situation." *It worked. His chest is defined handsomely.*

One is about to speak but the queen speaks first as she stares at him. "Advise me of my status in these unusual circumstances." She then focuses her eyes once again on the young chesty man. One tries to gain the queen's attention with a rehearsed speech. In a monotone, he says, "Your honorable one. We instigate under the guidance of our gods and the kingdom of the queen to start the investigation into our legal history to determine the approach bewith upon this situation. "

The queen hates not understanding the verbose cattle "sheff" that spews from the mouth of the LAD. "Please present your case as if you are speaking to a young child. I will not tolerate any sheff or any similarly foul-smelling garrulous raping of my auditory canals. Do you pontificate my assertion Head Legal Lead of the whatever in the whoever, fellating the Olympus of hierarchical doctrine BLAH garbage, sheff, sheff, sheff, sheff, SHEFF, SHEFF?"

The entire legal team except One lets out snickers and smiles. One has the look on his face of having receiving a well-placed kick to his briefs by the boot of a god. One is tempted to ask for clarification to the queen-invented word "sheff," but he chooses to remain silent, focusing on restating his presentation.

The young lad Pilastama speaks out of turn. "There have

been a few cases where the umbilical cord snapped during baby extraction. This is still seen as a great omen that the baby will be a great king, queen, thinker, builder, or any profession deemed respectful."

The queen waves her right hand, gesturing for immediate silence. The sunshine gleaming through the open windows starts to fade as clouds shadow the palace. "Continue, young man," the queen says. She keeps her eyes focused on One to prevent any further outbursts from him.

The young man gains confidence, knowing his legal teacher will not interrupt. "Because the baby achieved so long a distance, you, my queen, are bound to be seen as the living symbol of true motherhood. In all honesty, your power would become absolute."

One cannot hold back his breath; he speaks with venomous disregard to his future. "You are giving the queen political opinion, not legal! My queen, he is an underling with no understanding for protocol."

"Then is he wrong?" the queen asks.

"Well, I only concentrate on legal not political matters."

"Silly man. If you did not consider politics, then you have no business in this court."

"My queen, the law guides us all. Even a queen must follow the law."

"And law is filled with politics, is it not?"

"Philosophically, yes, but—"

"But what?"

The two go back and forth, bickering over the conceptual issues of kingdom law and tossing in the occasional curse word. If anyone had walked into the room without understanding the situation, the assumption would be that One and the queen communicate as if they are bonded by the law ritual of marriage.

When there is a gap in the debate, Pilastama speaks. "Because the baby has not been found and has escaped the presence of the court in a dangerous fashion, the people of Ovulum could summarize that the baby is dead."

Tears erupt from the queen, and a LAD gasps. Pilastama has no concept of sensitivity—his words scar the queen's soul, as he continues. "My queen, from what I was told, you unnecessarily exacerbated the birthing process with chemical concoctions. Your self-propelled royalty extraction trickery may be seen by the people of your kingdom as a power grab at the risk of harming a baby. You may lose your position as queen unless the baby is found immediately." He pauses slightly, noticing the flushed faces of his colleagues. "The baby must be found alive," Pilastama says.

A few hours pass with no sign of the baby. Just outside the court chambers where the queen's baby was born, a young man diligently holds an unusually shaped bluish-purple device. He waves the device in front of a guard, trying to persuade anyone within earshot that he can help the queen find her baby. A servant to the queen hears the commotion and approaches the young man.

"Please, guard, sir, I can help the queen. My Invisible Violet Infrared Light (IVIL) device can detect invisible liquid spills. I believe I can follow the liquid trail of the baby. I use this machine all the time in our industrial factories to detect deadly chemical leaks."

"Go away, fool boy," the queen's guard says, then grunts threateningly.

Although the queen's female servant is disgusted by the young man's oddly patterned peasant robe and discolored, sickly skin, she is intrigued by his claims. "What is your name, son?" she asks politely, although she is superstitious and tries to avoid his "poverty aura" by keeping her distance.

The young man and the queen's guard break their confrontational gazes to look at the well-dressed and well-endowed woman. The guard smiles at her beauty, and the young man takes a step toward her, while she steps back to maintain distance.

"Woman, do you have influence with the queen?"

The servant does not appreciate his boorish dialogue. She maintains her composure. "I do. What is your name? Explain your desire to see our gracious queen." She smiles back at the guard.

"I am Ein-Tolk of the Exploration Group, worker to the—"

"Enough. Explain your purpose to our generous queen," she says imperiously.

Ein-Tolk repeats the information he offered to the guard. He also tells the woman that his machine can be calibrated to search for invisible liquid spills in hospitals. Ein-Tolk adds, "With the right fluids, I can find the slime trail of the bouncing baby."

The servant knows the crude Ein-Tolk will probably upset the queen with his blatant disregard for protocol involving the queen's internal fluids, yet she knows that her high position in the court needs to be maintained and her court adversaries impeded. *The queen's problem needs to be solved, regardless of protocol.*

The female servant guides Ein-Tolk inside the court chamber and gestures to Ein-Tolk, signaling that he should be very quiet. She whispers into his ear, "My name is Queen's Servant Jordain Ananoset Irp. Tell me anything you want before we talk to the queen."

As Ein-Tolk whispers into her ear, Jordain shrugs her shoulders and shakes her head in utter contempt. When he is finished, she speaks with regret. "Let us hope she won't kill you on the spot."

"You may try to find my baby," the queen announces to her court. Ein-Tolk is ecstatic after his short presentation. He has convinced the greatest power in the kingdom to trust his skills and his device in finding the heir to the queen's throne.

"I have sent bounty hunters, officers of the court, trackers, pet owners pretending to be animal trackers, and various other professions to search for the child," says the queen. "I must admit that your approach is unique and unusual. Let us hope my decision brings positive results."

Jordain had educated Ein-Tolk on what should and should not be said to the queen. A sweat bead trickles down the side of

Jordain's face as her nervousness begins to show. Standing beside the queen's bed, Jordain kneels to whisper into the queen's ear. After a few minutes, the queen rubs her temples; her head is bent backward as she wonders, *Why do you curse me, gods?*

The courtroom of over twenty servants, guards, and political representatives quietly watches the queen as she lies back on her padded red throne bed, contemplating her next move. Jordain whispers again but is harshly stopped with a faint slap to her mouth.

"*Fine!*" the queen snaps, highly agitated. Everyone jumps at the sudden outburst. The cultural minister's bead necklace breaks by the sudden pull of her hand as the queen shouts. Small round jewels bounce and scatter wildly across the courtroom floor. "Everyone, get out!" the queen orders, and then points to Jordain and Ein-Tolk, adding, "Except you and you." The cultural minister's face shows distress as people walk out of the room, crushing the small jewels underfoot. Some women giggle at the cultural minister's embarrassment, as the crunching noise tells the court that her colorful jewelry was nothing more than an elaborate fake.

"Guards, leave as well!" the queen demands. Normally, the guards would comply but they are hesitant because of Ein-Tolk, a complete stranger to the queen's court. "I will be fine. Please give me privacy," the queen says.

The queen's guards slowly leave the room while staring harshly at Ein-Tolk. Ein-Tolk understands the message in the deadly gazes he receives.

Ein-Tolk's device has a small gauge and a few circular buttons fastened to a heavy plate of purple metal. At the top of the gauge is a small branch-shaped extension that gives the machine purpose. Using a fluid comparison fed to the device in Learn Mode and by sampling and scanning the perimeter, Ein-Tolk believes his machine can find the trail. Unfortunately, this Learn Mode would violate every protocol a queen should never experience. Yet her maternal instincts and political ambitions drive her to accept great personal ridicule and discomfort.

"Approach my bed, scientist," the queen says with dark overtones as she throws away the bed covers and props her legs into birthing position.

"Well, I am not really a scien—" Ein-Tolk says, then gasps at the nakedness of the queen's baby cannon. He expected something more, something different. Physically, the queen is a woman like any other woman, with the same plumbing.

"Don't gawk; just do what you need to do!" the queen says quickly. Her tone is shrill and slightly frightened. "Use that thing to get what you need."

The device's branch extension enters Learn Mode, as well as a private area of royalty experienced by few. Ein-Tolk presses a few buttons and observes the gauges, and his manner changes from optimism to doubt. "Hmmm," Ein-Tolk says. "If only my device could detect more afterbirth, then I could begin the hunt."

The queen raises her right leg higher and thrusts the ball of her foot into Ein-Tolk's face. He flies backwards, hitting his head on the off-white polished floor while his device exits Learn Mode and softly lands on the bed.

"*You fools!*" the queen screeches contemptuously. "Jordain! Show this man the sacred afterbirth!"

"Y-y-yes, my queen." Jordain grabs the device and then reaches under Ein-Tolk's shoulders to hoist him up. Both move quickly to a doorless chamber parallel to the main courtroom. The calligraphic sign etched on the wall left to the room access reads "Recent History."

Jordain removes her hold on Ein-Tolk. "You never told me it was afterbirth you needed!" she hisses. Ein-Tolk looks to Jordain in confusion as he holds his throbbing head. On a mantel is a clear glass jar full of a murky, grayish-red chunky liquid. Dangling from the mantel is a beautifully written sign, held by a golden string: "Queen Curranstashiustolvirginnot Life Pool for the_____."

Nothing else is written, but a space is left blank for words to be added in the future.

"Is that the queen's true name?" Ein-Tolk asks, while trying to decipher the cryptic and extensive personal title. "Curranstash—"

"Yes. Never reveal this knowledge, or your life will meet with misery beyond your expectation." Jordain drops the device onto Ein-Tolk's lap.

"Fine, fine. And what am I looking at?"

Jordain says nothing, leaving Ein-Tolk to solve his own question.

"Wait! Does that jar contain the queen's afterbirth? You actually keep stuff like that?" Ein-Tolk asks as he stands straight and grabs his IVIL device.

"Yes. Use that purple thing to get what you need. Be careful. The queen's afterbirth is considered a national treasure."

"I ... uh ..." Ein-Tolk stops speaking and proceeds to teach the device what it needs. He removes the thin glass cover from the jar and dips in the branches of the device. Immediately, the device beeps, signaling the completion of Learn Mode, and registers its readiness for the search. Ein-Tolk wipes the cold sweat from his sore forehead with his left sleeve. "We are ready to look for the baby," Ein-Tolk says with relief as he waves his device jubilantly.

When Jordain and Ein-Tolk return to the main courtroom, everyone turns to look at them, as if nothing awkward had happened earlier. As Jordain scans the faces of her adversaries for their reactions, Ein-Tolk stares at the gauges of his device, looking for the baby trail. By waving the device back and forth, he finds a starting point and an end point. Ein-Tolk scurries to the window where the queen's baby aerially left in a hurry earlier. Jordain gives a smug smile to her court rivals, knowing her discovery may fix her presence in future royal administrations.

Ein-Tolk waves his device just outside the window. The afternoon sun struggles to cut through the red and blue clouds that decorate the sky. "I see the trail! I see it!" Ein-Tolk says as he intently stares at his device. Court political leaders hurry to see the gauges and the window exterior. Only Ein-Tolk can interpret the device and the invisible trail.

The crowd murmurs various comments. "What do you see?" "Where is the baby?" "I can't see anything."

Ein-Tolk ignores the crowd. He is too busy containing his excitement at the discovery, along with his participation in this historic event. A rooftop on the left has a splotch of fluid, and then farther down, another roof has the same impression. Ein-Tolk turns and burrows through the crowd which has gathered behind him. The queen shows no emotion as Ein-Tolk approaches her bedside. "I found the trail, my queen. May I begin my exploration to find your baby?" Ein-Tolk asks.

"You may," the queen says. *I was going to execute this intrusive Ein-Tolk fool for his ignorant violation of my physique. I will withhold my decision to see if his ambition and device can secure my future.* The queen orders her guards to follow Ein-Tolk and to carry her bed as they search.

Ein-Tolk starts to descend the imperial mountain. He follows the hidden trail, one afterbirth stain after another, as an entourage of royal servants and the queen keeps pace. The mobile bed, which was hastily constructed for the queen to travel, becomes difficult for the guards to navigate through the narrow streets of her kingdom. After a quick vomit, the queen rearranges her travel methodology. She is to be carried on the shoulders of the two tallest guards, paired together.

Many dwellings cling to the mountainsides, along with narrow paved roads that spiral uniformly along the mountain interior, with confusing tunnel entrances and exits. The bouncing baby had by-passed normal navigation routes by using the rooftops.

Ein-Tolk and his followers come to the top of the extremely flamboyant imperial road hill. If anyone wishes to visit the imperial palace, this road is the only publically accessible method. As far as the eye can see, the tree-lined barricades decorate the length of the road. Pressing a few buttons on his baby-detecting device,

Ein-Tolk sulks slightly—the bouncing baby had found the perfect trajectory to roll centrally down the road. Any deviation could easily tear flesh apart as it hit one of the many weapon caches or large trees along the route.

"We must go down the Imperial Road," Ein-Tolk announces to the crowd. He proceeds downward. Without hesitation, his entourage follows.

The crowd grows substantially larger and eager to see the possible discovery of the baby who could be high royalty. Roughly an hour passes before Ein-Tolk notices a slight deviation of the trail. Again, luckily for the baby, it missed numerous objects that could kill any person instantly.

Ein-Tolk reaches a point where the edge of the road has a deep slope that leads toward the World Pools. He cannot understand the information he is reading on the gauges. Focusing his eyes on the surrounding environment, he sees a strange outline in the distance, just over the embankment.

"There!" Ein-Tolk yells with relief. He proceeds carefully down a steep hill that is connected to the imperial road. He runs between the World Pools until he reaches a freshly created wall. The crowd follows, mostly stumbling and rolling down the hill that Ein-Tolk scaled earlier. Many slow their pace, trying not to fall into the barricade-less pools of circulating fluid, which represent window access to other worlds. The excited baby-finder bellows with pride, "Boy-king hit this wall, ricocheted upward, and—"

The queen interrupts harshly, "*He?* How do you know my baby is a boy?"

"I am quite confident your baby is a boy. Look there." Ein-Tolk points to the fresh new wall. "See? Your baby hit this wall. Notice the unquestionable impression on that surface."

The queen shudders as she looks at the unusual pattern but changes her face to a wide smile, with tears streaming down her face. "That ... is that my son's outline impressed against this wall?" The wall has a significant imprint of a small person with five limbs. "This wall has been plastered recently so the surface was still wet and quite malleable when the baby boy hit the surface at high speed," Ein-Tolk says while poking his finger into the wall. The fingerprint he leaves behind gives Ein-Tolk the long-associated legacy he so desires. *I truly did it. I can now die without regret.*

One person from the crowd yells back to the others in the mob, "The baby is indeed a boy! The baby is a boy-king!" The crowd moves closer and coos at the prominence of the imprint. The little girls in the crowd cannot help giggling at the unusual impression on the wall. A young woman whispers to her friends as she makes a measurement gesture with her arms, "For a little boy, he certainly has the composition of a big man." The queen overhears the whisper and gasps, then laughs and kick-forces her shoulder transportation to turn away from the crowd, while her hands clasp her face. She realizes by the writings of prophecy on the walls that her son may be the true universal god. She tries to remember the claims. *Fresh strength comes from an unbreakable soul. From the endurance of a journey of hardship, one discovers a new universe to conquer.* She elates into her undergarments. Her shoulder-guards feel the wetness but remain soldieresque.

"The baby must have fallen into this World Pool," Ein-Tolk says sadly. The crowd of royalty and peasants moan with sorrow. "The prodigy boy-king must have entered another world, where only exploration experts can maneuver through the swirling tides without being lost to the World Pool rapids."

"Fetch me the Keeper of the Pools," the queen says while holding back her tears. She knows the chances of finding her son are very small, yet prophecy gives her hope of his survival. A few minutes later, a well-aged and experienced gentleman, wearing multiple-pocket forest garb, arrives under escort of the queen's troops. He ceremoniously bows and asks the queen for an audience. She shines to his ancient chivalry, but she is impatient for answers.

He speaks in a smooth but aged voice. "My queen, as you know we monitor the World Pools to observe the development of inferior races, to determine if they acquire, learn, invent, or create cultural or technological advancements that could complement our own."

"What are your latest conclusions of this World Pool?" the queen asks while pointing to the unfenced grayish-green swirling pool, which smells of roses and sewage.

"Questionable," he replies.

"How can 'questionable' be a reasonable answer?" the queen asks.

He sighs. "We have many other pools that have promising progress. This one is very difficult to understand. It could give us something new and spectacular, or it could just waste our time. The World Pools Exploration Society recently decided to build a wall around this pool to entomb this world so our resources could be used for more promising pools."

"Enough. This World Pool is now designated as a royal heritage site. Prepare the necessary people to enter this world to find my son. Stop construction of the wall." The queen sees the wall outline of her son. "That wall is now to be worshipped. Prepare this area to accept followers to pray for my ... our baby's safe return."

The crowd murmurs with questions. The pool keeper is breathless but quickly recovers. "But ... but your baby could be dead, grown up, or a monster to the inhabitants. We physically change to the individual World Pool environment in unpredictable ways. We may never know how to identify your son. Even if we find him, we need to find a way to bring him here." He pauses to rub his forehead with his arthritic left hand. "My queen, to find your son will take significant resources."

The queen shakes her head in agreement. "Then let it be done." She adjusts her voice to address the large crowd. "This boy-king may bring us into a new age. Our kingdom needs another golden diamond age and he will lead it." At the back of her mind, she can sense her power slipping as the people frown.

Chapter 1
Diagonal Protrusion

A man awakens, standing, holding a sword adorned in red goo, his insides burning, all clothes missing, five dismembered bodies crowding his feet. *I wonder if this is normal.* He looks at himself. Green, gray, and red impressions laminate his body with the peculiar precision of someone's rolling on a floor, engaged in a fight. His mind begins to speak to him. *A room full of slaughtered dead.* He notices a torch flickering patiently on the far wall. *How peaceful.* Pausing and staring stupidly at his surroundings is his new hobby. *I wonder if I have a name.* He grows bored and feels the need to move. *I have seen others use their legs to modify self-location. They call it "walking."* Step by step, he re-learns leg movement and escapes his stationary prison. The man's face hits the floor as his sword gently falls, cutting a corpse's eye. "Aaaaaaah!" says the clumsy man. His eyes study the red goo oozing through his corneas. He speaks to himself through his bruising lips, "Hello, floor." Blood bubbles with each breath. "Red goo does not like walkers." He rolls over, lifts himself up, and slips again. His knee snaps a bone from one corpse as his body lands on his side. He sees a foot. He tastes. He brings his own left foot to his mouth.

A few hours later, the funny tingling from his foot is gone—

licking his foot is too fun to ignore. *I will remember to do this again in the future since red-goo sucking cured the pain in my stomach.*

There is a person in the corner of the dimly lit brick room, staring blindly at nothing. The corner person never changes his expression. Sometimes he blinks his eyes, moves a hand, or wobbles in place, waiting for external interaction. The confused clumsy man slithers on the bloody floor and moves close enough to speak with the stiff, barely animated person. He stands up, trying not to repeat his previous slippery collapses.

The stiff person continues to look past his shoulder, not acknowledging his accomplishment of standing in place without falling. The blood-covered imbecile moves in closer, not realizing that he pokes the stiff man's thigh with his burly extremity. "Hello, weary traveler," the stiff man speaks. "Are you lost? I am the merchant Valtan. I do hope my wares satisfy your trading needs." The merchant Valtan still stands and stares straight, again acknowledging nothing.

Is my name Lost? The naked man pauses. *Why is this body part of mine protruding so diligently in a diagonally upward direction?* He bellows excitingly to Valtan, "Hello! Could you tell me …" He pauses to compose his desire. *What do I want to know? Ah, yes.* "Could you tell me who I am?" says the confused man to Valtan.

Merchant Valtan stares at nothing.

"Merchant Valtan, could you tell me who I am?"

Merchant Valtan continues to stare.

Remembering his previous discussion, he activates a conversation by poking Valtan's thigh once again with his diagonal protrusion.

"Hello, weary traveler. Are you lost? I am the Merchant Valtan …"

Losing his patience, he takes the back of his left bloodied hand and flings it across Valtan's face. A big slap echoes throughout the dingy room. "Answer me or face death!"

His mind races with questions. *Why did I make a threat like that so suddenly? Why does he keep calling me 'Lost'? For now, I suppose my name is Lost.* Lost does not know what to do, and he is not sure which incident shocks him more—his uncontrollable action of instant violence or Valtan's lack of conversation skills. His violent action teaches him so much. *There is a part of me I might not control.* He continues to ponder the possibility that the environment around him might pull out his hidden true nature. *Maybe I am evil. This might be fun.* Lost repeatedly whacks Valtan with his diagonal protrusion, believing his actions are a form of communication. Each contact with Valtan only extracts the same static response. *Perhaps Valtan is cursed into programmed servitude.* Lost grows bored and is convinced he will learn nothing more. "Good-bye, Stiffer Valtan." Lost kisses Valtan on the cheek. Valtan's eyes show fright, yet it is unnoticed by Lost. Lost moves carefully over the corpses, reaching the wooden stairs.

The naked foot-licking man, now self-proclaimed as Lost, finds other Stiffers in the village from where he woke. "Stiffer" is the only name Lost can devise to explain Valtan's behavior. The bright sunshine, the tall fluffy trees waving in the timid breeze, the simple wooden homes in the village all remind him of a chaotic past. Yet details or clarification of previous experiences before Valtan are absent.

Lost begins his investigation with the villagers. With each diagonal protrusion poke to a Stiffer, he learns a new name and repeats dialogue from each village resident. Some villagers do not have much to say. One woman giggles; others bow and bonk their heads against his diagonal protrusion. After everyone human-like in the village is treated by Lost, he communicates with the cats, sheep, pigs; nothing is untouched until a young boy appears from behind a building in front of a road near the bakery. The boy stops and stares at the baker's treats in the open window that tempt his appetite. Lost nonchalantly walks to the small boy and nudges his diagonal protrusion into the cup of the boy's ear. The boy swats at the irritant, believing an insect or small animal demands his attention. As the pokes became stronger, the boy turns his head to see the image of a naked, blood-covered man with a disturbingly hair-covered communication extremity. The boy can't scream. The shock overwhelms the young lad, and he collapses to the ground.

Hm-m. That is new. Lost looks down at the boy's face, which demonstrates agony, fear, and shock. Lost waits for the boy to recover, expecting the Stiffer curse to inflict this young one. The young boy remains collapsed for some time as the shadows of a late-afternoon sun grow steadily.

Lost grows bored waiting and decides he needs more coverage for his naked body. He walks around the village, randomly removing garments from the villagers—a shirt from a woman named Val, boots and undergarments from his first friend, Valtan, and pants from an older man named Mayor Jelk. Before he can wear anything, he hears a wailing scream from the forest. He drops the garments and runs toward the noise.

Lost sees a large person-like creature who is weeping, moaning, and fixating on a blackened, rotten tree. The creature wears short pants that barely support the enormous muscles covering every bit of the agonizing mass. Lost approaches slowly, wondering if this is another Stiffer like Valtan. He stops and looks down at his own diagonal protrusion. Lost is limp. *It is as if this body part of mine has a mind of its own.* With his primary communication tool down, Lost feels he is stuck. *How can I talk to this hurt creature?* Lost ignores the communication gap and studies the problem. *One arm stuck in the rotting tree. The hand of the creature is dusted with wooden slivers. A good punch was the creature's motivation.*

The creature moves a bit, taking a breath, and reveals his right arm, his left foot, and his head. All these body parts have been smashed through the wooden entrapment. *What makes a creature do this to himself?*

The creature senses someone is close. "Heeelp!" the creature cries. "Heeelp! Heeelp!"

Lost replies, "Greetings. Need some help?"

The creature responds while whimpering, "Y-y-yes, heeelp."

Lost is ecstatic. *Finally I have found someone to share words and exchange ideas.* "I will help." Lost walks to the creature. He pauses and then moves around the tree. *How did this creature get all his arms, legs, and head caught? Hmmm. The bark and wood has closed off the creature's escape route. It presses against the creature's skin as he tries to retreat. Cutting would take too long; amputation is problematic and so is fire.* Lost devises a new approach to the problem. "Friend, I will help you. I want to ask you a question. Can you answer a question for me?" Lost asks in a calm tone.

The large creature calms slightly. "Yes."

Lost is hesitant to use his plan, but he has to try. "Friend, who do you hate the most?" When there is no reply, he repeats the question slightly louder.

"*Blantor! I hate Blantor!*" The creature erupts with venomous bile as his hairy skin begins to turn pinkish-red.

Lost has no knowledge of this Blantor person. Yet the violent reaction from the creature gives confidence to Lost. *My plan might actually work.* Lost tells stories using Blantor's name as the evil main character. Lost emphasizes how mean Blantor is and how Blantor laughs as he does cruel things. The nasty stories soon pay off. Wood starts to creak and snap. Lost pretends to look behind the creature and lies, "Oh, hi, Blantor! What are you doing here?"

The big tree entrapping the large muscular man-thing begins to fidget.

"Blantor, why are you so close?" Lost asks.

The tree explodes as the creature frees himself from the wooden shackles. "I will kill Blantor!"

Lost waves his arms furiously in the air, trying to attract the attention of the towering creature. "Friend, friend, friend, be calm. Blantor ran away. You scared him," Lost says.

The creature frantically turns in circles, looking for any trace of Blantor. He sees no Blantor. He sniffs the air, trying to catch Blantor's scent. Sniff after sniff, the creature can find nothing in the air. The creature focuses on Lost.

"You are free," Lost says and smiles. Although the creature is free, it is cut quite badly all over its body. "We should wash your woundghhhahh," Lost says, but the words became garbled as the creature picks Lost up by the waist and holds him like a cradled baby. The creature runs and stomps full speed through the forest singing, "DuHero, DuHero. You are Du-Heeero!"

DuHero? Lost likes the new name, as he had nothing to lose, except the name Lost.

Chapter 2
Goons and Manbabies

DuHero, formerly known as Lost, arrives at a burned-out village on the left shoulder of his burly new friend. As DuHero is placed on the ground, bum-first, he notices a ferocious battle surrounding him. Dozens of men and creatures are heavily engaged with one another, thrusting weapons and throwing punches. DuHero looks for a method of escape, but his big friend blends into the battle. DuHero stands and watches the battle around him.

I am in the middle of a destroyed village. Why do these creatures fight one another? He giggles, noticing his lack of battle attire. *I do not think anyone would want to fight a naked man.*

A human-looking entity notices DuHero, smiles murderously, and starts to run toward DuHero. The angry man swings a small sword violently as he closes the distance. DuHero is not scared; he dodges the running man, who promptly falls on the ground, face-first.

The silly fool outran his own balance. DuHero ponders his emotional status. *I feel no fear. In fact, I feel exhilarated!*

The entity recovers and thrusts his small bloodless sword toward DuHero's belly. DuHero dodges again, tightly grabs the hand holding the small sword, and with a swift chest kick, removes the arm from the now stumpy, flying man. DuHero pries the sword from the dead fingers and places the small weapon firmly into his right hand. DuHero barely notices a flying axe heading toward his left shoulder. With a quick movement of his left arm, the axe slices and stops in the bruised flesh of the angry man's dismembered arm, held by DuHero. DuHero throws the arm up slightly and grabs the axe handle. A tall, pig-like, burly creature stomps toward DuHero, who is shaking off the severed arm from the axe. *Why must my diagonal protrusion expose itself so diligently during this fight?*

DuHero is tempted to sever the personal nuisance but resists the thought and has no time to fix his predicament. DuHero jumps high into the air and gracefully sits on the shoulders of the charging pig creature. The sword in DuHero's possession finds a placeholder in the pig's right eye socket, as the creature keels over dead. DuHero grabs the large mallet dropped by the pig.

DuHero goes on the offensive. *Anyone carrying a weapon is food for my blade!* Every kill DuHero makes is unique and morbidly artistic to onlookers. *I am skilled! In fact, these creatures barely challenge my capabilities.* After killing dozens of weapon-wielding creatures, he notices that previously slaughtered enemies are back, seeking vengeance. *I love their tenacity, but I am certain I killed them!*

DuHero looks to the ground to find a match between the living and the dead. *There! Their bodies lie at my feet but another of them shows? Do they have twins? Triplets?* Bodies start to stack as more and more revenge-driven creatures seek DuHero's attention. DuHero is becoming tired as more solo battles commence and more previously killed enemies appear. His exhaustion begins to show as DuHero's breaths become deep and strenuous. *I am surely going to die in the near future.*

As DuHero cuts the throat of another duplicate competitor for the fourth time, he sees in the distance one of his violent foes flung a great distance into the air and away from the fight. As more creatures unceremoniously fly away involuntarily, DuHero's motivation sinks into his chest, and he sees eight cloth-wearing giants approach his position. Creatures initially slain by DuHero are trying to reach DuHero, but the giants block any further confrontation.

The fighting in the village ends.

Every creature in the vicinity looks at DuHero. The giants circle DuHero. DuHero drops his weapons, preparing for the worst. *I want to fight, but I feel there is no need.* "I am at your mercy!" DuHero says, while avoiding eye contact with everyone.

A giant outside the circle shoves his way inward, smiles, and rumbles out a call, "Duuuhheeeeeero!"

DuHero looks up and sees that the bellowing creature is, in fact, his wounded, tree-smashing friend. DuHero's big friend picks him up, kisses his face, and clasps DuHero's body into his loving arms. DuHero is hugged like a long-lost cuddly toy in front of homicidal killers.

DuHero does not enjoy the pinches to his bottom. The other giants gaze at DuHero while a few feel the need to touch DuHero quite inappropriately.

"Duuhhheerrooo," one giant coos.

"Duuhhheerrooo," says another giant, with a large scar on his face.

"Let me pass," growls a voice beyond the wall of giants. The wall of giants opens and a normal-looking old man with blazing orange hair walks into DuHero's view.

Worry traces its influence on the wrinkled faces of the concerned. This man must have great responsibility.

"What do you call yourself when you are alone?" the man demands.

"Lost, usuall—ugh!" DuHero groans as the giant shifts his hugging strength.

"Manbaby," says the man, as he plants a delicate hand on the giant's thigh. "Please put the nice, violent, naked man down."

Manbaby complies, and DuHero falls to the bloodied earth.

"What is your name, stranger?" the orange-haired man asks.

"That could be difficult," DuHero replies. "All I know is … hmmm. Well, I appeared in a room full of dead bodies and a village of lost people, like myself." All eyes demand a better answer. DuHero jumps up and with each jump, he says a word. "I … do … not … knoowwww!"

The humans in the crowd laugh. The Manbabies remain motionless but smile contently. DuHero's little hopping dance makes his diagonal protrusion wobble profusely. "Duuhheeerooo!" the Manbaby snarls.

DuHero looks around. Dozens of creatures still gaze at him intensely, demanding an answer so that they can remember this event and know who caused the commotion.

"Let us call me DuHero." DuHero, formerly known as Lost, formerly known as nobody, smiles.

"My name is Flagrot," the old man replies as he rubs his left ear. "Why did you come to our training village and attack us?"

"That Manbaby, as you call him," scolds DuHero while pointing to his big friend, "brought me here and dumped me in the center of your dispute. It was you creatures who started attacking me."

Flagrot winces at DuHero's nudity. "Young man, you are certainly something. I admire your gall. It is not every day that a powerful warrior with no clothing or memory is dropped into our village and kills us Goons multiple times. You must be a recently Awared Goon. Welcome to our Goon training camp."

DuHero is slightly relieved, knowing he may find answers to his identity. But then he pauses in his mind. *I killed dozens of these Goons. Why would I learn anything more if I am killed? Perhaps Goons have a system of justice where I may survive a deadly punishment. That orange-headed fellow did welcome me.*

"How did you get the Manbabies to protect you?" Flagrot asks.

DuHero looks to his big injured friend, who is smiling from ear to ear.

DuHero slightly smiles back. *Can I escape? Are these big-men*

giants my new friends? Why do I have the urge to suck my foot?
DuHero's racing mind is disrupted by Flagrot's next question.

"Manbabies do not volunteer their trust to Goons, let alone
protect them vigilantly. What makes you so special to gain
protection from Manbabies?"

DuHero ignores Flagrot and walks to his Manbaby friend.
"Thank you for saving my life." DuHero softly projects his
kindness as he places his comparatively small left hand on top of
the Manbaby's large left hand. "Can I call you a friend?"

All the Manbabies' faces immediately shine with excitement
and happiness. The surrounding non-Manbaby Goons are shocked.
The Manbabies became surprisingly joyous and begin jumping in
the air, imitating DuHero's previous actions. The ground rumbles
as each Manbaby pounds the earth with his enthusiastic weight-
filled springing. Flagrot rolls his eyes.

"Afffriend! Afffriend! Afffriend!" Every Manbaby repeats the
phrase, while some stop jumping and randomly pick up a Goon
to give a crushing hug.

Once the excitement dies down, Flagrot continues his inquiry.
"I assume you did not know what you just did?"

DuHero turns to Flagrot, but before DuHero can respond, his
wounded buddy picks up DuHero and hugs him. Flagrot speaks
louder, assuming DuHero cannot hear through Manbaby muscle,
which is cupped against DuHero's ears. "Manbabies do not have
individual names! You just gave that Manbaby a name!"

DuHero speaks in a muffled tone, as his mouth is pressed to
the Manbaby's left breast. "I ... I did not give him a name. I only
called him a friend." DuHero's legs dangle in the air as he tries to
wrestle out of the Manbaby's affection. Again, all the Manbabies
sing, "Afffriend! Afffriend! Afffriend!"

Flagrot continues, "You just called that one 'Afffriend.' That
Manbaby will try to use that Afffriend name for the rest of his
life."

DuHero is still confused and disorientated with the strange
culture of these Goons, Manbabies, and those other un-named

creatures in the surrounding crowd. *What did I get myself ...
ugghh ... this beast is strong and smells like my rear end.*

The Manbabies modify their song. "Duuhheero, Afffriend,
Duuhheero, Afffriend." As they sing, green spit flies all around
the training site as the "ffff" part of the Manbaby ceremonial call
blankets the embraced DuHero.

I strangely feel ... I feel ... happy?

An unorthodox, wet friendship is born.

The warriors whom DuHero had slain earlier laugh at the
slimy engagement. "Be quiet, Goons!" Flagrot scolds.

DuHero is a bit shocked upon hearing the word "Goon" once
again. *I know that word, Goon. What am I feeling? Confusion?
Anger? Pride?* DuHero is not sure what he is feeling, but then his
thoughts turn to the feeling of friendship with Afffriend. *I will
take this feeling, even if I do not understand it fully. What is my real
name?*

Flagrot resumes the discussion. "The Manbabies here have
given you the name DuHero. At the same time, your Manbaby
friend is now called Afffriend."

Afffriend had briefly put DuHero down, but when his name is
mentioned, Afffriend quickly grabs DuHero by the shoulder and
pulls him in for another loving embrace. DuHero appreciates the
physical affection, but it is starting to hurt. DuHero cautiously
speaks to Afffriend. "Thank you, Afffriend. But no more hugs,
please. You made me too happy, and I may explode if I get too
much."

Afffriend understands and releases his battered friend. Flagrot
is impressed but does not show any emotion. Flagrot's mind
ponders the circumstances. *Manbabies can be hard to control.
They are strong men with the emotional stability of a baby and thus
ideally named. But DuHero has them tamed, in control.* Flagrot
looks to the sky and notices the lateness of the day. "It will be
dark soon," Flagrot announces to the crowd. "DuHero, please be
our guest and join us at our city tonight. I assure you no trouble
will come to you."

Before DuHero can respond, Afffriend picks up DuHero by the head.

Snap! Afffriend has broken DuHero's neck. DuHero dies instantly.

"Duuhhheeerooo!" cry all the Manbabies. The Goons slowly back away from the mourning Manbabies. Afffriend tightly hugs the broken body of DuHero. "Duuhherroo!" they continue to bellow loudly. Some Manbabies jump up and down while others pound the ground with their fists and heads. Those who pound their heads began to lose consciousness and weave wearily among their mourning peers. The Goons continue to back away, except Flagrot, who carefully approaches Afffriend.

"Afffriend!" Flagrot says authoritatively. The unexpected funeral ceremony drowns the air with yelps and howls. The sounds become deafening. "Manbabies, be quiet!" Flagrot screams as loudly as he can, yet his orders are not heard or obeyed. He continuously repeats his demands for quiet until most Manbabies turn to silent weeping. Flagrot is able to speak at a normal tone. "Afffriend, it was an accident. Nobody is blaming you." Afffriend continues to clench tightly to DuHero's carcass. Large tears run down Afffriend's face and soak DuHero's blondish straight hair. The drenched hair glistens in the setting sun. "Afffriend, place DuHero's body over there," Flagrot says as he points to a burned-out small house. "We can protect DuHero so he can pass and come back to us."

Afffriend slowly walks to the designated charred burial plot for DuHero. Afffriend respectfully places DuHero's body against a wall so DuHero's body looks like he is just resting. Afffriend slowly walks away.

Flagrot designates assignments. "Goons, we are guarding DuHero's body tonight until his next self appears. Manbabies, go to the graveyard and wait for DuHero."

Without hesitation, all the Manbabies run toward the graveyard that is located just outside the village. A Goon asks, "Why are we protecting this flaggot?"

Flagrot, expecting this type of question, has an answer. "DuHero is one of us." Flagrot raises his voice so more Goons can hear. "DuHero has already won the respect and protection of our Manbaby brothers." Most Goons nod their heads in agreement. Some Goons move to the house containing DuHero's body and begin forming a perimeter of protection. A few Goons remain with Flagrot.

Flagrot sighs. *I need to be ready for more questions. Being an accountable Goon can be straining to the imagination sometimes.* Flagrot continues to observe the Goons following his orders. *Sometimes I wish accountability was not part of Goon culture. But in an extraordinary sense, the philosophy seems to work. It's strange that other cultures do not adopt it.*

A Goon approaches Flagrot and makes a loud and unfunny comment. Using a well-rehearsed magical chant, Flagrot promptly decapitates the Goon with a few musical words. The Goons laugh as the Goon head bounces to the ground and the headless body flops backwards.

Sometimes it is great to be a Goon.

Chapter 3
Goonerocity

Q ueen Ovulum reviews a summary report of the Questionable World Pool.

The land of Forever, a large almost rectangular expanse surrounded by distant oceans, contains a dominant culture in each corner of the land. Goons, an irreverent culture with self-entertainment ambitions, control the northwestern portion of the land, while the Snobs, a human-like race with a strict hierarchal and militaristic structure, control the northeast. Nymphs, an all-female–creature queendom, shares most of the south with Porcs, a pig-like race. The boundaries are unclear at this moment. Between each of these major kingdoms is an informal neutral zone, an almost lawless area, where creatures and cultures can interact without any interference of home customs. This zone also contains many creatures called Boortards. These selfish creatures can take on any role of the other four kingdoms, camouflaging themselves to cause trouble and mayhem for personal gain.

She crumples the parchment into a ball and throws it at the fire raging in the fireplace, missing her target.

*　　*　　*

DuHero awakens, wiggling his body with confusion in his eyes as he witnesses the wobbling backside of some strange creature.

"Hrmphh," the creature grunts.

Flagrot walks slowly to look at DuHero, who is slung over the shoulder of the Porc creature. "You are right, Tabby," says Flagrot as he tries to look into DuHero's upside-down eyes. "DuHero, Tabby is carrying you back to our village. Try not to struggle."

A few dozen Goons wearily follow behind Flagrot and Tabby as the parade of tired soldiers follow a dirt path, which is barely lit by the seven moons in the dark-blue glowing sky.

With every heavy step that Tabby takes, DuHero's face slightly bumps into Tabby's large posterior. DuHero is not concerned with the touching but with the terribly awful smell. DuHero tries to arch his back, only to see undesirable splotch stains embedded in Tabby's pants. The stain resembles the horrifying crushing experience of a small animal that did not know when to run.

"Can … can I be put down?" DuHero asks, wincing and trying to turn his head away for fresher air.

"Stay still. You are very weak and cannot walk after dying seven times," Flagrot says while trying not to laugh.

DuHero is still distracted by the smell. Flagrot chuckles as DuHero tries to turn his nose away from Tabby, only to be met by the same pungent scent. DuHero just takes notice of the news of his multiplicative demise. *I died seven times?* "Is dying many times normal?" DuHero wearily questions.

"How long have you been Awared?" Flagrot asks.

DuHero pulls his left arm inward to cover his suffering nose. "I do not understand," DuHero says.

Flagrot raises an eyebrow. "From your clueless response, I must assume you became Awared quite recently, so your memories have not returned. I will answer questions later. For now, enjoy the ride to my home."

Tabby expels something gaseous and insufferable very close to DuHero's nose. Flagrot notices the stench and quickly talks to DuHero. "Welcome to the land of Forever. Enjoy your sleep. He-he."

DuHero groans incoherently and immediately becomes unconscious.

"Yalta's bean broth again, Tabby?" Flagrot asks in a muffled voice, while covering his own nose.

"Hrmph!" Tabby snorts.

"Bring him to my hovel, Tabby," Flagrot says as the Goons separate and head to their personal destinations within the city of Pink Bosom. Tabby picks up the pace and passes Flagrot, who is contemplating his upcoming conversation with DuHero. Tabby reaches the home and promptly dumps DuHero's sprawling body on Flagrot's front step.

"Thank you, Tabby," Flagrot says as he steps over the slumping body and enters the modest but protrusive home. Tabby walks away swiftly, with no concern for anyone.

"Tabby, oh Tabby, what will I do with you?" Flagrot mumbles while grabbing DuHero's shirt. Flagrot drags DuHero's unconscious body into his home and toward the flame in the fireplace. DuHero begins to open his eyes, groans, and notices the wooden architecture everywhere he looks. Flagrot's home is typical of Goon architecture—spheres and rounded cylindrical objects of complementary arrangement decorate the walls and furniture, all in varying colors and materials with phallic arrangements. Colored vials, sealed glass beakers, and many books diligently occupy any available shelf space.

"Did I die again?" DuHero wearily asks.

"No, just a nasal assault called Porc and Beans," Flagrot says as he reaches into his cabinet for dried meat and herbs. "You have a big day tomorrow. The Manbaby you call Afffriend has reached self-awareness and has accepted your assigned name to him. He will need to attend city court council to determine if he deserves a name. Your presence at the trial may help him."

"Everyone deserves a name," DuHero responds as he rubs his forehead. The pain of today's events still bangs on his skull. He stands and notices the large wooden table with a comfortably padded chair. He sits down on the chair and releases a comfortable groan of spontaneous relaxation.

"DuHero, I do not believe you understand Manbabies very well. Manbabies are men with baby brains, as their title implies. Not even normal babies are self-aware until many moon rises have passed. Self-awareness is a challenge for our big brothers." Flagrot continues babbling as he puts meat and herbs into a pot that is cooking on a pale fire. "I suppose your name, DuHero, was something the Manbaby gave you?"

"I suppose. I do not remember my name, let alone anything or how I came to be here." *What did I just say? My head really hurts, and my back end feels assaulted. No, no, I won't think about it. Ow! My skull!* "Why did I die seven times?" DuHero asks.

"Oh, my mistake. It is eight now. Tabby used your body like a spear and flung you head-first at a white rabbit—Tabby has an irrational fear of little cute animals—and inadvertently broke your neck. We picked up your new body at the graveyard, still unconscious and naked."

DuHero can now justify his headache. *What about my back end?* "What … err …. who is Tabby?"

Flagrot sniffs his cooking brew and nods his head. "Not ready," Flagrot whispers, then speaks normally, turning to face DuHero. "Tabby, better known as the Angry Blacksmith to Goons, is from the Porc territory. Simply, he is a pig-man who became a Goon. We had Tabby carry you, as you are quite a muscular, heavy fellow. Only Tabby could pick you up."

As DuHero looks at his right hand, he notices he is wearing a long-sleeved gown. "I am dressed," DuHero says.

Flagrot smirks while turning to his boiling pot. "You are an unusual one. Of all the creatures that die and recover at the graveyard, you are the only one who seems to appear naked.

Everyone else who dies wears at least a few pieces of clothing when they re-exist."

My nudity is not normal, yet coming back to life is normalcy to Flagrot. In DuHero's mind, the concept of his re-existence is significantly more important than a little vanity. *Death is usually permanent, in my thinking.* "Why can I die and appear at a graveyard?"

"It's natural, just like the two suns and the seven moons. Death is a wonderful settler. The life board is cleared of another bothersome pawn. The graveyard is part of life and death and life again," Flagrot says with ironic overtones. Flagrot takes a small sip of the soup and smacks his lips in satisfaction.

"It just *is*?" DuHero philosophizes.

"Correct. It just is."

DuHero's eyes begin to focus on his surroundings. The unusually tall house has a long chandelier that lights the small home quite well. "Are you a fancy cook or something? There are unusually shaped bottles and glowing items everywhere. Am I a cook? What am I?" DuHero smells the soup. *Now that is a fantastic smell.*

Flagrot brings the soup to DuHero and slightly drops the bowl, causing a "thunk" sound on the table. "I have interests in everything," Flagrot says.

DuHero grabs the bowl and gulps the hot broth. *I suppose when one is hungry, anything tastes and smells fantastic. This could be a bowl of festering dog intestines, and I would probably still engorge myself with Flagrot's soup.*

Flagrot watches the horrendous consumption of his soup, which now partially covers the table, chair, floor, DuHero and, surprisingly, a bit of the high ceiling. "You are certainly not royalty at the dinner table," Flagrot says while searching for a rag to clean the mess. "I suppose you are a cross between warrior, jester, and insanity." Flagrot finds a worn cleaning cloth and brings it to DuHero. "I think you are a Goon."

DuHero finishes the soup and belches proudly. "What is a Goon?"

Flagrot sits down in a chair not covered with soup. "Long ago, the other cultures threw out undesirables from their societies. We were classified as Geographically Ousted Ones Not Suitable. We formed our own community, focused around the discrimination and our behavior, and we fought back. Goons culture was born."

"How does that relate to me?" DuHero asks, while leaning back comfortably in his chair. "I might have a Goon history. Or I may be a new person to this world."

Flagrot is a bit surprised at DuHero's clarity in personal assessment. "Well, individually a Goon is an irreverent and conflicted individual who goes against all protocols in the name of self-fulfillment and a cheap giggle. We are more of a cultural behavior than a race. Goon society is made up of all races— Nymphs, Snobs, Porcs, and sub-races, including Manbabies." DuHero stares blankly at Flagrot. A small drop of soup hits the floor, breaking the silence. Flagrot sighs and continues. "In simplistic terms, the men and creatures you killed at the training grounds—they are Goons. Goons are a bunch of jesters, clowns, and assorted individuals who can't take life seriously. Goons live to be amused, and that is why they were fighting with one another earlier."

"Battling each other is Goon culture?" DuHero asks.

"It is difficult to describe Goons. If you get it, then you are probably a Goon at heart." Flagrot sits at the table, facing DuHero. Pride shows through Flagrot's face. He truly loves being a Goon. "We are a culture of comedic freaks with deadly weapons who love to instigate amusing hardship on others."

DuHero makes a face of triumph. "So due to my behavior, you believe that I am one of you? A Goon, you call yourselves?"

"Yes," Flagrot replies with a hint of hopeful understanding in educating DuHero. "I believe you became Awared quite recently;

therefore, your behavior is certainly understandable … and quite amusing to Goons."

"Awared? You mentioned that before."

"Awared is the name given to those creatures like you who came out of the slavery curse. You can see those who are cursed by touching them, and they repeat the same words over and over again."

"I call them Stiffers. I saw them at the village, not far from our fight."

"Not a bad name. These Stiffers, as you call them, are used by the Boortards to buy items, sell spoils, acquire tasks, gain rewards, and other things we do not fully understand."

DuHero sighs. "And who are Boortards?"

"Creatures which look similar to us but are controlled by a god, mysterious entities, or some other unknown methods. Their primary motive seems to be self-serving—greedy beings with bloodlust and tyranny flowing in their veins. They vary in strength and skills but overall are extremely dangerous."

"How would I recognize these Boortards?"

"They are not very smart but certainly ambitious. They don't talk; most of them hop around like idiots. They wear unique armor according to their desires and mostly, they congregate around Stiffers."

"So how are they different from Goons?"

"Good point," Flagrot says as he cracks a smile. "You will understand when you meet one. If you see a group of Boortards, keep your distance. These beings are extremely powerful if they have good leadership." Flagrot changes the subject. "I am amazed with your unification with the Manbabies. They are not easily influenced, unless it's screamed into their ears."

"So Manbabies are Goons?"

Flagrot smirks. "Well, yes and no. They are Goons to us." Flagrot makes a strange hand gesture to emphasize the word Goon. "But they do not have the same rights as a regular Goon. Our entire existence is based on our Goon culture, and Manbabies do not 'get' our Goony ways. Manbabies do not receive the same respect and laws from Goon society. We know Manbabies are like us Goons, but Goons victimize our big brainless cousins."

"Isn't your behavior toward them wrong?" DuHero asks.

"Wrong is defined by those who do not wield power," Flagrot says with relaxed zeal.

"I suppose I will right some wrongs as the days progress," DuHero says while leering at Flagrot.

"You might just do that. But that is a big political battle and—"

DuHero interrupts Flagrot by darting toward the open food cabinet. DuHero promptly consumes anything edible he can find.

Flagrot laughs. "You are such a Flaghat, DuHero. Stop eating all my food."

DuHero stops chewing on a brick of cheese, turns to Flagrot, and asks, "Flaghat?"

"Flaghat, flaggot—there are many terms to represent curse words, which were integrated into our language after the spectacular Goon conquest during the Flag wars from the past. The word "Flaghat," in this situation, is a person whose behavior is rude and blatantly impolite, yet not that serious."

DuHero puts his left hand on his still-aching head. *So much to learn.*

"Flaggot is a word dominant in Goon language and possesses many meanings and derivative mutations into other words and actions. Every Goon is a Flaggot, and every Goon action has a level of Flaggotry."

DuHero's mind wanders. *This guy sure loves his Goons.*

"Those Goons who are giant Flaggots, not by physical size but by actions done, are either well respected or widely hated. These Flaggots perform acts of raising Goon culture, through drama and exceptional negative or playful actions against an enemy, or integrating a contribution widely discussed, amused, and accepted among Goons. No other race can figure out Goon culture, let alone speak our reference-based language."

DuHero pretends to understand by nodding his head. He begins chewing, grabs a few pieces of bread, and walks back to the table and sits. Bits of cheese and bread fly out of DuHero's mouth as he speaks. "Why did I die so much?"

Flagrot roars with laughter. Tears flow down the wrinkly crevices of his aged face as he tries to overcome his laughter. "I … I am sorry," Flagrot says. He wipes the tears onto his sleeve. His laughter turns into a gulping giggle. "That Manbaby you helped—what was his name? Ah, yes. Afffriend—he loved you so much that he killed you multiple times."

"You mean he loved to kill me?" DuHero says in amazed confusion.

"No, not at all. Remember what Manbabies are? They are babies with the aptitude and strength of a very strong man—wildly emotional and extremely dangerous if not handled properly. Heh … like some women I know."

"Oh, yes, now I remember." DuHero smiles a bit. "Afffriend grabbed me, and all I could remember is severe pain around my shoulders."

"Yes. The Manbaby accidently broke your neck. He wanted to carry you."

DuHero ponders the experience. "I do not remember anything except waking up on that pig creature's shoulder."

"We call him Tabby. You might have forgotten our earlier conversation." Flagrot wipes his own face, clearing any remnants of his previous belly laugh. "He is a Porc by race but a Goon by culture. Or so we believe. A peculiar and very mysterious creature." Flagrot tapers off into silent thought but eventually returns to his dialogue. "Memories before and after death can be difficult to recall. The memories may recover if someone tells the person what happened or if something or someone unlocks the experience. Again, another strange condition that the gods ruled in the matters of life after death."

DuHero finishes the last of the food. "I still do not remember. Tell me more."

Flagrot shifts his thin body into a more comfortable position. "After death, your body meat is left behind, along with any possessions you carry. The closest graveyard usually spawns a new body with your soul inside. The re-existing time is not immediate; sometimes it can take hours. In your case, it did not take long." Flagrot lifts his hands to cup his face. "Now that I think about it, the whole experience of your continuous death was just a farce. I do not know how Goons can function the way we are, but we do."

DuHero's right eyebrow lifts, announcing to Flagrot that he wants the story, not the philosophy.

"It took us a while to convince Afffriend to let go of your dead body. We convinced him to walk with us to the graveyard. You appeared, strangely, naked. Everyone else who re-exists at least is given minimal clothing."

DuHero rolls his eyes. *Yes, old man, I appear naked at graveyards. Why is it such a fascinating mystery?*

Flagrot says, "The god of the death-to-life expanse must continue to miss you in the redressing ceremony."

DuHero yawns. *I should learn more about these gods, but I am too tired to care.*

Flagrot smiles and continues. "Afffriend saw you standing there and ran toward you. Afffriend tackled your second self and crushed your body."

"So now there are two dead me's with Afffriend?" DuHero leans on the worn table, trying to contemplate his unknown participation over the past day.

"Yes," Flagrot says. "Afffriend and his fellow Manbabies were completely puzzled, while the Goons couldn't stop laughing at the incident." Flagrot pauses, then giggles. "The Manbabies thought the Goons were pulling a cruel joke on them. A big fight broke out between Manbabies and Goons. As swords were swinging and skulls were being crushed, you appeared back in the graveyard."

Flagrot laughs and can barely keep his composure. "The third time you died, it was from a Manbaby falling backward onto you. Your fourth death was from a wild sword swing from a Goon. I do not know how your fifth and sixth bodies died, but we found them among the piles of dead Goon and Manbaby bodies."

DuHero's eyes light up. "So ... since the Goons and Manbabies died at the graveyard, they kept reappearing and prolonging the battle?"

"Ha-ha-ha-ha-ha-ha!" Flagrot laughs at reliving the Goonish memory of the recent past.

DuHero's feelings are mixed. *I want to smash Flagrot in the face with my foot, but Flagrot is helping me understand this strange existence in these Goon lands.* DuHero withholds his anger.

"Goons become extremely excited over these bizarre circumstances. Lots of emotion, lots of action, lots of destruction!" Flagrot's voice increases in pitch as he stretches his body, making creaking and popping noises from aging body parts. "It took us hours to fix the mess, but it was glorious!" Flagrot continues to laugh as he stretches.

DuHero does not like being the center of humor at his expense. *How can such a tragic event stir such elation?*

As Flagrot lowers his arms, DuHero clenches a fist but resists the urge to catapult his displeasure into Flagrot's experienced face. "Tragedy makes Goons happy?" DuHero murmurs.

Flagrot's laughter subsides. "No, not just any tragedy—comedic tragedy." Flagrot pauses and notices the anger in DuHero's face. Flagrot carefully continues. "Listen, DuHero, this is just how we are as a culture. Goons came from a past that is filled with horror, hopelessness, and self-doubt. In our own comedic tragedy, we learned to overcome our potential demise by embracing the injustices of life by laughing at its cruel rule-set."

DuHero again makes a face of confusion.

"That's how we are; embrace your culture!" Flagrot says as he reels. "And put your fist away. I can probably dodge any physical blow you attempt on my feeble body." There is an uneasy pause of action in the room. The flame in the chimney starts to dim. Flagrot stands up, walks out of the room into another part of the hovel, and comes back with drab-colored blankets. "You can sleep over there," Flagrot says, pointing toward the corner near the flame. He throws the blankets on DuHero. DuHero catches the gray fur-like blankets, walks to the corner, and tries to get comfortable. Flagrot leaves the room again. A few minutes later, Flagrot runs back into the room where DuHero is resting. Flagrot has heard the horrendous, beastly noise of the dreaded Dilhadren, a vicious creature that makes the sounds of rumbling mountains, bubbling lava, gurgling streams, and spraying geysers. The room is dimly lit by the small fire in the hearth. Flagrot studies the room carefully, looking for any sign of the creature or DuHero.

Where is that creature? Where is DuHero? Does he not fear the vicious noise, or did he run away? The noise erupts again. Flagrot spins around, trying to find any indication of where the creature is going to attack. Flagrot's ears point toward DuHero. Flagrot relaxes his guard, focusing on the thought that DuHero could be a Dilhadren. Flagrot walks slowly toward DuHero as the noise echoes profusely from DuHero's big lips. Flagrot pauses in shock. *That Flaghat snores like …* Flagrot's thoughts taper off as another loud snore rocks the house with tiny yet noticeable stuttering vibrations. "DuHero snores like the sound of a vicious Dilhadren," Flagrot mumbles as he sits down at the table. *What in God's power created this DuHero?* Flagrot laughs a bit as he prepares for a long, sleepless night.

Chapter 4
May Goonocracy Thrive

"It felt like I was flying. I looked toward the ground, and I saw this twisty shape in the mountains," DuHero says. DuHero uses his fingers to draw the unusual shape in the air. "The symbol was huge, and it kept growing and growing—like I was gliding toward a painting being brought to me. Then everything went black."

Flagrot asks DuHero to draw the symbol in the dust on the window. The double-lined twisted symbol gives Flagrot a tremendous feeling of discovery. Some more details are shared between them and finally, Flagrot has a good idea where this symbol is located. Flagrot's mind races with excitement. *DuHero's first memory could lead Goons to a glorious future, and I will work to make it happen. So much to do, so much! So much, so much, so much …* "Go explore the city and learn more about Goon culture," Flagrot says. "I have numerous tasks I need to complete." He grabs parchments from a nearby desk and begins sketching frantic self-instructions.

"Sure. Let's hope I do not kill too many Goons," DuHero says with a partially joking overtone. DuHero steps outside into a summer morning and into something squishy on the ground. He scrapes the foul substance off his donated boots with a rock.

DuHero then wanders aimlessly between the unusually shaped buildings. Flagrot's home is tall, slender, and smooth. The round patterns on the walls look wooden, yet distinctly fake and barely natural. DuHero can see familiarity, yet the shape remains a mystery. Beside Flagrot's home is another tall, slender building but with hairy moss growing from it. DuHero continues to study the many buildings that surround him. Then DuHero understands what he is seeing. *They all look like my diagonal protrusion, except homier.*

A fisherman walks by and gives DuHero some wisdom. "It's not how deep you fish; it's how you wiggle your worm." The hardy seaman walks away, chuckling at his own joke.

DuHero suddenly feels arousal around his intellectual shortcomings. His attention is drawn to other Goons near him. A few Goons practice acrobatics, some fix their homes, and one is teaching a group of children. Surrounding the children are many small empty seats in the form of metal benches, fresh-cut wooden logs, and anything that can support a posterior. DuHero sits on a wagon with a broken axle and missing a wheel, just outside of the pile of chairs and children. As the children sing a short tune, spectacular things happen. One child chants a song, and a frog appears on a classmate's lap. Another child chants the same tune, and another frog appears.

"Can I learn what the children learn?" DuHero speaks out to get the male teacher's attention.

"You mean the chants?" the teacher replies.

"I suppose."

"Chants are mysterious voice-triggered actions, unique to the land of Forever," the teacher lectures. "The children learn minor chants so they can survive in the wild, in case they become lost."

"Yes, that is what I want to learn," DuHero says.

"You are welcome to participate and learn, as long as you accept being a victim to experimenting children. Watch and learn from them." The teacher pauses to see if there is room for a large man to be with the children. "Come sit over here. I expect you to learn and participate on both receiving and sending chants."

DuHero nods and enthusiastically sits on a small chair among his shorter peers. As DuHero listens to the children, he tries to replicate their linguistic chant patterns. "CrEaTe WaTeR," DuHero says as a mangled chant. Instead of a good mug-size portion of fluid, a puff of water vapor appears. A faint belief in usefulness and capability rushes through DuHero's body. *I did it! I can create water. Well, the misty kind.*

"My name is Chinny Chin," the teacher says. His slanted eyes draw attention from the battle fought between his hair and his ever-increasing baldness. He is much shorter and skinnier than DuHero but certainly commands authority from the kids. "What is your name?" he asks, while looking into DuHero's eyes.

"DuHero. I am new to this city and … well, new to this world, I suppose." DuHero continues to explain his circumstances to the interested teacher.

"Ask me any question you wish, DuHero. I will help any way I can. *HEY!*" The teacher focuses his attention on a young blonde girl with an extravagant smile. The teacher scolds the mischievous pupil. "Be careful where you focus your chants, young one. I do not appreciate my pockets being filled with water." The students laugh and then silence quickly. "CrEaTe WaTeR!" Chinny Chin chants in a dominant tone. A huge ball of water, the size of a small house, appears over the head of the shocked, ill-behaved girl. Gravity drops the water punishment on top of her, soaking her thoroughly. "LiGhT ZaP!" the teacher says, and the girl jolts from her seat and falls to the ground. All the students except DuHero roar with laughter and point to the electrically shocked student. She smiles at the incident and takes her seat. Her wet hair covers most of her eyes, but this does not stop her from gazing at Chinny Chin in an adoring manner.

"Young lady, sometimes I think you like being punished," Chinny Chin says.

"Chinny, tell me about this land I am in," DuHero says.

Chinny turns his attention to DuHero. "You are in the land of Forever in Goon territory in the city of Pink Bosom, Pustuous District." Chinny Chin notices DuHero does not understand how to aim his chants. "Watch the children's hand gestures. While they chant, they think and point to the location where the chant should appear."

DuHero tries to follow his instruction but the bulky novice is constantly distracted by the continuous soaking of water by the children—now reaching the sixty-seventh soaking.

The teacher resumes his summation. "Although many of the creatures of Forever do not need food and water to survive, eating and drinking is important to sustain our bodies to full energy and stamina. Not having food or water means sluggishness, laziness, and much slower healing."

DuHero watches as Goons pass by the school; he tries to master more chants. He notices Goons seem to be mostly man-type, but the children have equal sexes between males and females. DuHero has no fear in asking Chinny Chin questions not related to chants.

The teacher accommodates the big pupil's curiosity. "We have a children exchange program between Goons and Nymphs. Both races feel the children need to see many perspectives between their cultures to grasp the differences that separate them." DuHero's further inquiries lead Chinny Chin to patiently reply. "Nymphs are mostly female-type creatures. They have their own culture and values that do not conform to Goon standards. They respect the Goon culture's ability to be creative and inventive and to accept one's defects and weaknesses and turn them into strengths. Goons do not have the skills of nurturing, respect, or discipline, which is needed for young children. Both races decided long ago to geographically separate Goons and Nymphs to focus on their strengths, prevent frustration, and reduce fighting between the sexes."

DuHero wants to learn more history, but he is distracted by ten Goons, who look like soldiers, entering the area not far from the school. The guards ask questions to random Goons, out of earshot of the pupils. In the distance, a Goon points a finger toward the class. All the soldiers approach DuHero.

"Are you DuHero?" one soldier asks.

DuHero nods yes.

"You are under arrest, DuHero. Please come with us without question."

DuHero slowly stands. "Thank you everyone," DuHero says. Then he waves good-bye to the kids as he walks away from the class. "CrEaTe WaTeR!" DuHero chants, while turning and trying to aim his hands toward the school. He successfully wets all the children with an uncoordinated water spray. They laugh at the surprise and wave good-bye to DuHero as he is escorted away.

DuHero finds himself guided into a dark room. The cell door closes behind him, and his mind begins to panic.

I truly hate enclosed dark. DuHero has no visual or auditory sensations as he paces carefully around his small lightless room to measure his range of freedom. *This space is not enough.* The reason for his incarceration never enters his thoughts. DuHero closes his eyes, trying to calm his racing mind. *Keep it together, please. Sanity, please.*

There is not enough sanity. Painful familiarity feeds his fear. DuHero slaps his face over and over, just to hear the noise and possibly see the pain. His soul gives him hope on memories he never knew he had, such as the loving, soothing grasp of a woman. *A familiar hug could seal the cracks in my spirit ... I think.*

He does not know how much time has passed. This short incarceration gives him a lifetime of enclosed fear. *Nothingness.* Nothing reminds him of the vast world outside the jail. His inner prison is crushing any remnants of his humanity. He prays. *What is praying? I have seen this ceremony for desperate people seeking quick fixes.* DuHero rubs his face with both hands. *How do I know so much?*

"*Memory return to me!*" DuHero yells with maximum strain

to his lungs. He makes a fist with his left hand and punches the ground. His knuckles become bloody from continuous repetitive blows. *Memory, why do you hide like a scared rodent? Are you a rat? A cowardly rascal?* "What are you? Where are you?" No one responds to his calls. *I think madness has come to my pity party instead of memory. I will call my new friend … Mie.* "Hello, Mie, my mistress of madness. Can you find my rat-fearing friend called Memor-ee? He-he-ha-ha-ha-ha-ha-ha!" DuHero is amused by the unintended rhyme. "Oh, Memoree?" he coos, as if he's searching for a hiding plaything. "Where are you Memoree? I will find you, Memoreeeeeee." *Ha-ha-ha! Oh, this game is fun. He-he! Well, it was fun.*

DuHero begins to chant words he heard earlier. Over and over again, dozens and dozens of times, he repeats the words. His benevolent-sounding chant is phrased as a prayer and uses the same tuned words as a "Create Water" chant.

The small jail cell quickly fills with water and DuHero drowns.

He is free.

*   *   *

Not far from Flagrot's home, gangs of Goons gather in a large rainbow-decorated arena to handle the immediate issues of the day. Posted on the wall is the docket of today's events:

No-confidence vote: *Removal of Dictator Ruler Boss Queen Hip Number-One Top Goon Flaggot Fathom Refailable (Some-one had scribbled in more unreadable titles, probably less flatter-ing than the misspelled published version.)*

Policy change: *To allow Manbabies to possess individual names*

Criminal Trial: *Goon Kingdom versus DuHero. Charges of lewd indecency, theft, and moral corruption*

The no-confidence vote is a daily occurrence. The vote is a way for Goons to continually remind the leadership that the population has the true power, not the politicians or cult-following personalities. For the 467th vote in a row, the motion to remove Refailable from power fails. The leader keeps his responsibilities, as the Goons laugh once again at their daily Goon theatrics. While the Goons in the audience talk amongst themselves, the Manbaby named Afffriend is guided onto the central platform currently surrounded by Goons. Across the hall on a separate stage, the judgment panel of seven Goons reviews the case and discusses the details amongst themselves. After short deliberation, one judge moves to a device to magnify his voice, which Goons call the Mini-Dong Mike, or dongmike, to honor the inventor of audio magnification. In a slight echo, the judge's test cough is heard throughout the arena. Goons, in their usual Goonish behavior, mock the cough with their own audience-wide echoes of coughs. Many coughs are followed by spitting and other noisy bodily functions. Goons know how to entertain themselves for any event.

"Okay, Goons, shut the holes in your faces," says the primary judge, self-named Jay Dee Cider, or as Goons pronounce it, Jay-Dee-Cee. Jay-Dee-Cee, a fairly ordinary looking fellow with no discernable distinction to his body, face, or clothing, speaks in a passive and slightly monotone voice. "Let me tell you Goons what's up." The crowd acknowledges Jay-Dee-Cee's authority by reducing the sound of their voices and fake coughing to a stirring murmur. "That Manbaby at the central podium was given an official name by a stranger. The name given is …" Jay-Dee-Cee quickly scans the paper he holds in his left hand. "Afffriend? Yes, Afffriend."

Afffriend looks up. He cannot pinpoint where his name is coming from in the crowd.

The judge calls out to Afffriend, "Manbaby. Manbaby!" The judge tries a new approach. "Afffriend. Look over here."

Afffriend turns and sees the judge. "Afffriend, me!" Afffriend says, correcting the judge and pointing to himself.

Jay-Dee-Cee understands and offers a small smile. *The Manbaby has taken that "Afffriend" name and is responding to it. This will not turn out well for him.* A judge from the panel calls to Jay-Dee-Cee and waves him to join the group. Jay-Dee-Cee walks to the polished cherry-colored table where the judges deliberate once again. They chat for a few moments and then nod in unison. Jay-Dee-Cee returns to the dongmike.

"The panel has reached a decision," Jay-Dee-Cee says, then pauses to take a deep breath. "Identity breeds distinction, which turns into independence and the demanding of rights. We do not believe Manbabies have the capacity to manage their future, let alone an identity. To maintain Goon civility and structure, the Manbaby known as Afffriend will enter re-education and learn to conform to the standard generalization of their race behaviors. In conclusion, Manbabies cannot have individual identities."

The Goons mumble, but no objections are called out.

"Guards, take the Manbaby away for re-education."

Afffriend is led away. The Manbaby is confused, which brings him to tears as he senses something is wrong. The Goons become silent—a rare occurrence.

*   *   *

Goon prison guards make their way to the jail cell containing DuHero. They open the main door, only to find the inside hallway filled with water that spills outward and cools their ankles. Water pours through the thin cracks between DuHero's cell door and the wall. A guard unlocks the damp door; the latch is pulled back with difficulty. Eventually, the door swings open, pushing the Goon guards down to the wet floor. DuHero's body bumps its way through the river-laden hallway.

"Check the local graveyards," says a guard with an authoritative demeanor. Guards storm out of the small prison.

A naked DuHero sits on a rock, eating an unfamiliar delight and waiting for the guards to acknowledge his presence. "Hi, guys! Want a sandwich?" DuHero holds his right arm out and offers his meal. The guards look at each other, wondering what the word "sandwich" means.

*   *   *

A fair amount of time has passed, as the Goons in the arena buzz with festive social chatter. Nobody minds waiting for the start of the trial of the Goon Kingdom versus DuHero. Some Goons try to sell goods, others put on a show, some debate, and a few are in friendly fistfights. On the stage, the judgment panel is just as sociable. One judge spits upward and catches his phlegm gobs in his mouth, badly. Goon prison guards parade a naked DuHero onto the judgment panel stage. DuHero is placed in a small cage, facing the audience, along with a dilapidated wooden chair. Goons laugh as they watch Jay-Dee-Cee remove one of his undershirts and hand it to DuHero before the Goon guard locks the door. DuHero places the shirt over his prominence as he stares at the large audience. Jay-Dee-Cee nonchalantly walks to the dongmike near DuHero's cage.

"Goons, stick a dong in it." The audience becomes mostly silent. "Goons, now will be the trial of the Goon Kingdom versus DuHero. The charges are lewd indecency, theft, and moral corruption," Jay-Dee-Cee says.

Goons in the audience look at one another with puzzled stares. They talk amongst themselves; a random dialogue can be heard.

"Lewd indecency? What haven't Goons seen?" one Goon says to his companion.

"True; we are experts. I didn't know a law was in place for typical Goon behavior," says another Goon.

Another Goon in the crowd says, "Your face is a prime example of lewd—"

"Shut your flaggotry face, flaggot." The first Goon replies, knowing the insult is directed toward him. A shoving match begins between the Goons.

"All right, enough!" Jay-Dee-Cee says into the dongmike. "Open your ears and shut your food stuffers. We will give you details."

During this time, Flagrot runs into the arena. He nudges through packs of Goons to the front of the crowd, where the judges are sitting.

"Accuser, please step forward and sit in the accuser's chair, facing the prisoner," Jay-Dee-Cee says into the dongmike, while pointing to the handsomely designed blue chair. The accuser's chair is comfortably padded with Snob kingdom luxury designs and crests. Known only to the judges, the conveniently stolen chair is used to support the Goon justice system by helping the accusers feel comfortable and treated with respect during a trial. From the audience, a small man carefully steps onto the forward stage and sits upon a comfortable-looking vacant blue chair, just outside of DuHero's cage.

"Hi, Valtan!" DuHero yelps with glee. The Goons laugh as Valtan falls back in his chair and hits the floor. Valtan picks himself up and sits, keeping a suspiciously careful eye on DuHero.

"Valtan, tell us what happened," Jay-Dee-Cee says.

Valtan tells the story of what DuHero did to him in the past, from the toe-licking to dong-poking, the face slap and then the kiss, then stealing his pants and undergarments. The Goons are roaring with laughter, along with a few judges.

"Are these claims true, DuHero?" Jay-Dee-Cee asks, with discipline in his voice.

DuHero nods yes.

Valtan interrupts with his own questioning. "I do not know how all those bodies ended up in the cellar, but it must have been DuHero's fault! You did kill those people, didn't you? Answer!"

"Bodies? Who knows of these bodies?" Jay-Dee-Cee asks the audience.

DuHero turns his head to see Jay-Dee-Cee. "Yes, there were bodies there. Yet I was not the one who killed them. Or at least, I am unaware of my past behavior."

Many in the audience miss DuHero's words. They shush themselves quiet. Jay-Dee-Cee looks to the judgment panel. They shrug their shoulders in semi-unison, knowing nothing about the dead bodies. Jay-Dee-Cee turns back to the dongmike. "Anyone who was killed in the cellar of the cursed village Startenpoint, please step forward," Jay-Dee-Cee says.

No one approaches the stage. A few Goons call out the name of a Goon who is well known for being blame-named (a person who is blamed for everything, regardless of circumstance or capability). The more improbable the person is to ever be involved, the funnier the name is to Goons.

Jay-Dee-Cee talks directly to a Goon over the dongmike, who is recording the trial on paper. "Aside from the usual asshatiness, please record no one who approaches the stage. Those who were killed automatically recuse their justice claim of their death in this matter. Therefore, the dead will receive no justice at this time because their living selves say nothing. May Goonocracy thrive."

"May Goonocracy thrive," the audience replies.

Valtan and DuHero stare blankly at each other in their unusual circumstances. The Goon justice system is beyond their comprehension.

Jay-Dee-Cee turns to DuHero. "DuHero, did you do the things Valtan claims?"

"Yes, except the dead bodies part," DuHero says with ease.

"The dead bodies are irrelevant," Jay-Dee-Cee replies.

"Then yes, I became Awared and did those things to the Stiffer Valtan."

A member of the judgment panel corrects DuHero's terminology and insists that DuHero use the "slavery curse" lexicon. It takes five hundred words of explanation for DuHero to finally understand. The audience is restless and rolling their eyes at the waste of explanation time.

"Oh, oh, I get it now," DuHero says. *They should have said "use slavery curse" and not "Stiffer." I didn't think Goons could show such complexity and legal verbiage.* "My apologies," DuHero says. "May I ask a question?" DuHero says loudly, facing the judgment panel so they can hear over the Goon ruckus.

One judgment panel member nods.

"Please, everyone. Quiet down," Jay-Dee-Cee says into the dongmike.

DuHero turns to Valtan. "Valtan, why did you not tell me to stop? You must have been Awared, yet you repeated the same sentence over and over again, like a cursed person."

"I … I …" Valtan struggles to reply.

DuHero hammers his argument. "Were you acting when I poked you with my diagonal protrusion many times?"

Goon laughter erupts with asynchronous coordination, as many spectators clue in to the meaning of "diagonal protrusion."

"Lexicon clarification: diagonal protrusion?" a judge asks, leaning into a dongmike on the panel's pink-draped table.

The audience yells, "Dong!"

The judges look at one another in lucent agreement. "Understood. Let the record show that the phrase 'diagonal protrusion' means 'dong.'" The judge leans away from the dongmike. "Like we don't have enough synonyms for dong." The panel smiles and snickers softly.

Jay-Dee-Cee turns to Valtan. "Please answer the question. When DuHero tried to communicate with you, why did you not respond?"

Tears fill Valtan's eyes. "I was trapped. I could not move. I was Aware but still trapped." Valtan stops to wipe his tears from his face, using his right hand. "Only recently was I able to run— run from the blood, the closure." As Valtan rambles on about his emotional state and other irrelevant personal experiences, the audience murmurs with uncomfortable observation. Panel members do not like where Valtan's responses are going.

"What did you do first after you became physically free from your bond?" a panel judge asks.

Valtan wipes away more tears. "I ... I ran around looking for someone to arrest that man." Valtan shakily points with intense fervor at DuHero. Beginning to feel further discomfort, the panelists shuffle in their chairs. A Goon judge, who has not spoken during this trial, interjects with his own questioning. "You did not stop to contemplate your new freedom? Did you not explore, talk to people, taste food, examine yourself, and look at the beauty around you?"

Valtan shakes his head. Flagrot waves to his friend on the panel. Flagrot's judge associate is dressed in a flowing blue silk robe with assorted vertical colored ribbons of distinction waving in the wind. As he approaches Flagrot, the judge kneels down on one knee and listens to Flagrot's whispered proposal. Manbabies begin pouring into the arena and sing, "Duh-Hero, Duh-Hero, Duh-Hero." Random Goons yell assorted obscenities to provoke the Manbabies. Occasionally, a Manbaby storms the aisle, grabs a heckler, and proceeds to throw the Goon violently through the roof to guarantee that the trouble-maker is displaced far from the arena. Many Goons fly that day. "Duh-Hero, Duh-Hero, Duh-Hero" continues to echo in the crowd. Their synchronic voice of protest lets everyone know who they do and do not support, as Goons violently exit the arena. DuHero sits in the uncomfortable wooden judgment chair in his cage.

The Goon judgment panel has never seen an organized Manbaby lobby on this scale. Goon after Goon starts to agree with the Manbabies. Slowly, the entire arena thunders, "Duh-Hero, Duh-Hero, Duh-Hero." Manbabies stop throwing Goons to their deaths. A judge asks the audience for silence. The Goon and Manbaby crowd grows louder. The panel sits back and waits for the audience to tire themselves. Flagrot's judge friend returns to his judgment panel colleagues and begins deep, private discussions.

The judgment panel waves to Jay-Dee-Cee to come for discussion. He complies. DuHero waves to the crowd and asks everyone for silence. Everyone complies. Jay-Dee-Cee walks over to the Grand Judgment Horn located on the far right of the large stage. The horn is immense and secured to the foundation, where one end is the size of a small mouth, and the tube gradually expands upward toward the ceiling. At the other end is a large mouth turned downward, facing the spectators. If the horn ever falls, the large mouth could swallow dozens of stacked Manbabies. Jay-Dee-Cee kneels, inhales deeply, and then expels a long breath into the horn. The crowd cheers, as a roaring growl protrudes from the large vibrating object. Goons clap their hands as the Manbabies jump up and down with grunting joy. The crowd knows more than DuHero can understand. The great horn becomes silent, then resumes with another boisterous roar. Everyone becomes silent.

Jay-Dee-Cee pulls his mouth away from the soaked part of the horn and points his mouth to the dongmike. "This Goon judgment panel and the community that surrounds you have made a unanimous decision. The person sitting in this judgment chair shall now be called Goon DuHero." Jay-Dee-Cee points to DuHero with calm approach. "DuHero, welcome to the Goon community. May Goonocracy thrive." Jay-Dee-Cee walks to DuHero's cage while changing his pointing hand to an open, welcoming palm. DuHero receives a quick slap to the head. The crowd roars, as DuHero is joyously confused. DuHero smiles as many in the audience raise their arms with open palms and flick their wrists, duplicating Jay-Dee-Cee's gesture. *The crowd acknowledges my existence.*

After a few minutes the crowd's cheering becomes a murmur. "Guards, please move close to the prisoner and the accuser," orders a judge, who sits sternly at the table. Jay-Dee-Cee has rejoined his fellow judges on a comfortable and quite stolen Snob chair of royalty. Shuffling and "uh-ohs" are heard from the audience. They know more drama is being prepared for their salivating Gooniness. The guards position themselves for action.

"This court has found ..." The judge pauses to deliberately increase the suspense. "This court has found Valtan to be a Snobby Flaggot. He demonstrates clear behavior of cowardice and ungooniness, and the Goon Judgment Council does not recognize his charges against DuHero. Guards, throw Valtan into the crowd so he can be torn apart." The mob cheers and sings as Valtan is hurled into the waiting hands of Goon justice. DuHero winces as chunks of Valtan pass over the crowd, like a toy bouncing on thick rippling mud. DuHero sees a Goon chanting Valtan's right ear and places the morbid reward in his pocket. *According to my recent schooling, that Goon used a Trophy chant. I wonder how much of Valtan's body, if any, will show up at a graveyard.* DuHero sees more Goons trophy-chanting chunks of flesh and bone. *Valtan, as I know him, is no more—that's my guess.*

The arena is now packed with Goons, Manbabies, and an assortment of creatures unknown to DuHero's experience. News has spread of the Manbaby riot, and Goons want to participate in the action. The crowd is rowdy but remains relatively civil with a party-like atmosphere. Multiple attempts by the judges to quiet the crowd have failed. A fat judge goes behind the scenes of the sitting judgment panel and guides a young boy to the stage. He sits down near DuHero, where Valtan sat previously, shaking with fear. The audience witnesses his fright and shushes themselves silent. Jay-Dee-Cee walks to a dongmike near the boy. The judge reads out the charges.

"This boy, named Torinos, has accused DuHero of lewd indecency and moral corruption. Torinos, please tell your story."

Torinos brings his small knees to his chin and cradles his legs with his arms. Nobody can hear him speak so Jay-Dee-Cee drags a dongmike close to the boy's mouth. Torinos's dialogue is broken and filled with hesitant claims. The judgment panel does not have any doubts of Torinos' authenticity of events. They summarize that DuHero had placed his diagonal protrusion in the boy's ear. They also accept Torinos' experience of spending the night alone in the cursed village of Startenpoint while Goons battled one another in the distance, further frightening the boy. His mother also was fearful of the battle noises and did not leave her hovel for fear of becoming lost in the dark.

"I still have nightmares of being alone in the dark, as noises of people dying fill the air," Torinos says.

DuHero explains his reasoning to the Judgment Panel. "I thought my diagonal protrusion was the only way to communicate to Stiffers." DuHero quickly learns from the chuckling judges that a simple touch from any body part is sufficient to alert a cursed person to attention.

Torinos says, with bravery and clarity in his high-pitched voice, "You stunted brain waste! You hurt my soul!" Torinos brushes a few tears with his right hand. "My mommy worries because I have not been hungry or happy after that night." Torinos's sobs become stronger. DuHero joins him with his own tears.

My actions caused so much distress to this boy.

"DuHero," Jay-Dee-Cee says with authority, "are all of his claims true?"

"Yes," DuHero replies, as he wipes his face with the donated clothing.

The audience is split, debating the story among themselves. The Judgment Panel talks for the length of two bean-filled expulsion bathroom breaks. Their major conflict is over the question, "Where does Gooniness stop, especially toward young impressionable children? Although DuHero was being Goony, he did it to a sensitive child." Ironically, being Goony to children is frowned upon by many Goons.

"I am sorry," says DuHero. Torinos faces away from the audience and DuHero. At this time, the Judgment Panel renders their decision of DuHero's fate. The fat judge stands and walks to the Grand Judgment Horn. As the Goon turns his voluptuous bottom toward the horn mouthpiece, the crowd roars in reserved objection. He places his rear end on the horn mouthpiece, grips his butt cheeks with his hands, and expels a horrible bowel-induced noise that would make even the great gods hold their noses in potential nasal irritation. The flatulent sound rocks the ground that surrounds the arena. The sweat beads on DuHero's hands wiggle to the vibrating, boisterous judgment of guilt. DuHero is found guilty by fetid obnoxious symbolism.

The Manbabies understand the judgment. Without regard to Torinos's damaged feelings, many of the large creatures chant "DuHero" over and over again. As his name starts to echo in powerful auditory unison, DuHero gestures to the crowd in a back-and-forth waving motion, hoping the crowd will silence. The observant audience complies, and the ruckus begins to mellow into random coughs and farts. Jay-Dee-Cee walks over to Torinos, bends over, and whispers into the young boy's ear. Torinos quickly stands and runs to his mother, who is watching in the dark shadows of the rear stage. Jay-Dee-Cee walks to a dongmike closest to the audience and nearest to DuHero.

"The Goon kingdom has found DuHero guilty of lewd indecency and moral corruption. The Goon Judgment Panel understands DuHero was recently Awared, and he did not understand Goon laws. Nevertheless, no Goon can claim ignorance in his defense." Jay-Dee-Cee pauses to gather the community's reaction. The crowd mumbles yet no objections are yelled out. Jay-Dee-Cee continues with his summation. "Tomorrow at City Hall at full sunrise, DuHero must demonstrate his Gooniness by singing a song to the crowd. Any other acts of Gooniness will be reviewed by this panel to determine if DuHero should receive further penalties. This trial is adjourned. May Goonocracy thrive."

The audience begins discussions, while guards release DuHero from his cage. Flagrot walks to DuHero and places his hand on DuHero's shoulder. "DuHero, come with me, and I will prepare you for tomorrow." They move through the crowd. Goons pat DuHero on his back, showing their support. DuHero is happily confused.

Chapter 5
Payment

DuHero spends the day rehearsing his repayment to Goon society. Night falls over the city, and the Flagrot home changes from merry singing to monstrous snoring. As morning comes, someone just outside Flagrot's home yells news of a woman approaching the area. Flagrot quickly throws on his drab clothes and walks outside.

DuHero rubs his sleepy eyes. He stands from his makeshift bed and follows Flagrot with curiosity. An outline of a strange creature appears in the distance. The far-off creature is in no rush and smoothly caresses the ground with her long, slender steps. Before DuHero can ask, Flagrot says, "DuHero, that is a Nymph." Her deep blue eyes stare straight over her recently broken nose, reset to sub-par normalcy. Every hip-step bounces the crossbow that rests on her side. She has the face of an angel but the stare of a brutal killer. Her skin-tight blue uniform is lined with assorted blades, insignias, and small body parts. Fingers, elbows, and pie-cut flesh gracefully bobble from side to side as she moves toward Flagrot. As she comes closer, DuHero notices that everyone in the area is locked intently on her presence.

"Should I be worried?" DuHero whispers to Flagrot.

"Juulia Estratra will be joining us."

"Why do the Goons—"

"They are in awe," Flagrot says, bluntly interrupting DuHero's next question. "They are indirectly giving their respect and sexual admiration to the presence of beauty and feminine strength wrapped in a Nymph uniform."

"I hope she's a good cook. I'm hungry," DuHero says with an unknowingly brazen attitude.

Juulia hears the insulting remark and sprints toward DuHero, wielding one of her body blades. Flagrot steps aside as DuHero casually dodges multiple attempts to cut his throat. The blades continue to whish around DuHero's evasive side-stepping. Juulia steps in close with a belly-thrust stab—a potentially fatal mistake. DuHero simply moves around her, grabs the trophy foot dangling from her belt, and rips the morbid treasure from its thin rope chain.

"Can you cook this foot, woman?" DuHero casually asks as he looks over the foot's condition.

Juulia stands still in shock. No man has ever dodged her attack, let alone removed her most prized flesh trophy from her being.

DuHero starts nibbling on the big toe and is disappointed. DuHero studies the foot once again. *My appetite wants this foot so badly, but I do not know why.* "What is this flesh? It has no taste and has the strength of hardened leather," DuHero says with comedic zeal.

"Return the trophy, DuHero," Flagrot insists.

DuHero flings the foot to Juulia. She catches the extremity, examines its condition, and proceeds to re-tie the morbid recompense to the belt over the cheek of her right buttocks.

"Flesh trophies are chanted into a condition to not rot, nor to give the previous owner access to the appendage again," Flagrot says.

"This is not just any flesh trophy!" she insists with spitting contempt. "This is the foot off a Snob High-Grace Guard."

"So?" DuHero asks.

Juulia's face cramps as she studies DuHero carefully with only her eye movement. She finds the perceived weakness for her next attack and lunges for DuHero's eye. DuHero bends downward as her arm extends over the missed eye. DuHero grabs Juulia by the throat with one hand and her crotch with the other. He lifts her high above his head.

"DuHero, that's enough!" Flagrot says with obvious displeasure. Juulia is in shock as she dangles helplessly in the air. DuHero casually dumps her flailing body on to the ground and strolls toward Flagrot. She winces as her backside aches and her pride is in tatters. The Goons witnessing the show hold back their laughter, knowing any sort of amusement from the incident will certainly be met by more feminine blades to their observant throats. DuHero looks to Flagrot without any regard to Juulia's presence. "My underpants need washing. Does she do laundry?"

Flagrot apologizes to Juulia for DuHero's behavior. DuHero keeps his distance, thinking about his manner.

Where did that brash attitude come from? I feel great! He looks over Juulia feeling no remorse or guilt. *That woman stimulates me in unusual ways.*

Juulia turns away from DuHero to reveal her solid shapely posterior.

I want that. I … I don't know if I want to grab it or kick it. Am I being Goonish?

Flagrot yells back to DuHero. "DuHero, walk to City Hall, and don't forget your costume or the song I taught you." DuHero waves, acknowledging Flagrot's instructions as he gives a smile to Juulia. She turns her head away in disgust. DuHero enters Flagrot's home, re-dresses and hums a song in his head.

The walk to City Hall is short. Many Goons from the audience of yesterday's trial are waiting for DuHero's penance. Jay-Dee-Cee walks to DuHero and guides the guilty man to a large stone stage near the City Hall main doors. The large stone stage is used for numerous justice decisions and occasional protests. Light blue wooden stairs beside the high stage allow two men, walking side by side, to reach the stage in safety. The judges from yesterday's trial follow, and they gather on the stage, blocking access to the stairs. Jay-Dee-Cee points to an area of the stage with a man-sized circle painted pink on the central stage.

"Are there stairs in your house?" Jay-Dee-Cee says to DuHero.

DuHero looks back without pause. "I am protected." The secret Goon code conveys his readiness as a Goon in the know.

"Good. Make it good and goony, DuHero."

"Yes, flaggot."

Jay-Dee-Cee smiles. The audience begins to swell and close any gaps near the stage. DuHero thinks about changing his act slightly by walking on the heads and shoulders of his audience, but instead, he looks to City Hall to verify that the ladder prop is ready.

DuHero begins serving his punishment. He reaches down, pulls a boot off his foot, and places the stinking apparel on his head. He sings the song that Flagrot taught him the previous day:

> *We are flaggots, a bunch of worthless scum.*
> *We are flaggots; the worst is yet to come.*
> *Dongs and butts and neck beards, stink and fat we are.*
> *We think we have the longest dongs to touch the stars!*
> *Raise your drinks, kill your friends, make us live for fun.*
> *Tease the Nymphs, punish the Porcs, kick Snobs in the bum.*

He sings the same verses a few more times, with horrendous mistones and off-keys. The Goons enjoy the act, regardless of how badly DuHero shatters any reasonable concept of good singing. As Goons begin a sing-along and cheer at his presentation, DuHero takes a bow, dropping his boot. He rises and announces, "I, DuHero, being of squandered mind and soul, declare my intention to take over Goon territory!" DuHero drops the rainbow-colored robe he is wearing. All that covers him is one boot and a flag with smiles and crudely drawn cute animals waving from his diagonal protrusion.

Goon kingdom leader Refailable smirks as he listens to DuHero's broadcasted news of the one-man mutiny. DuHero darts off behind the stage to an awaiting ladder that's leaning on City Hall. The audience roars with laughter as he climbs the ladder quickly and approaches the flagpole, which delicately holds the official flag of the Goon kingdom. While DuHero attempts to tear the City Hall flag down, Refailable pulls out his crossbow and aims for DuHero. The arrow flies through the air and pins DuHero's diagonal protrusion to the flagpole. DuHero grasps the flagpole and leans his body against it for support. He tries to stop the strange circumstantial pain he feels from his normally pleasurable manhood. Everyone laughs intensely at the unexpected participation of official Goon leadership in a regular sentencing hearing. Smart Goons know that any threat to Refailable's leadership, regardless how small and silly, is immediately quashed by Refailable himself, the attention-hungry fatso. The crowd screams, "Historic!" and "Epic!" and Goon terminology such as "Elollerfives!" to conclude this event, as it is significantly important to Goon culture.

When the judges stop laughing, they make their decision. "DuHero has paid his debt. Sentence served!"

"Justice is … quite … painful," DuHero whimpers.

*   *   *

News of the arrow's impaling reaches Flagrot and Juulia. Both run to City Hall and join the crowd, who are still laughing at DuHero's embarrassing situation. DuHero is in too much pain to pull the arrow out himself, and no one is willing to let the macabre display end.

"Why aren't you idiots helping him?" Juulia yells with contempt. She runs to the ladder and carefully approaches DuHero. She crouches and looks into the eyes of the suffering

DuHero, who is using all his strength to hold up his body to prevent tearing damage to his diagonal protrusion. She smiles as she grabs a small axe from her chest and waves the sharp, metal-sculpted flesh-dicer in front of his face. "I wonder which obstacle I should chop?" she says in an obviously threatening manner.

A look of horror fills DuHero's face as she raises the axe and aims for his predicament. The audience changes from laughter to saying, "Ooooohh!" followed by "Aaaaaaaouch!" followed by more joyous screams and laughing. She chops the arrow and a fleshy souvenir for her belt. DuHero is free but his manly pride is taken as she chants her new trophy.

Chapter 6
Pink Stink

DuHero spends a few days recovering from his injury. Alone, he sits at the main table in Flagrot's home, pondering his next move. *Should I march over to Juulia's temporary residence and ask politely for my body part back?* He pauses and shakes his head. *No. She probably hates beggars.* DuHero winces with pain, trying to accept his physical and emotional wounds. He forgets about his previous thoughts. *My missing manhood will not grow back unless Juulia releases the Trophy Flesh chant on my diagonal protrusion. How a small piece of man reduces manliness entirely.* He places his hands over his face to massage his morning beard, a project of mostly contemplation and part laziness. *My current priority is a prison break for my parted part.* He gazes intently at his memory of Juulia's face when she dropped her arm, which made the infamous slice.

How will I get it back? I cannot jeopardize Flagrot's wishes of maintaining peace. I want to know more about her but not have her hate me. Actually, I do not see her as a contemptible enemy. More of … of a challenge. Think, you fool!

DuHero paces in laps around the main table, occasionally bumping his hip into a misaligned chair. *A one-on-one fight might work. But if I lose, then there would be no chance of ever recovering it. I could steal the trophy … no.* He remembers what Flagrot told him. *The chant needs to be broken with a different chant by the original chanter. Think different; think original. Come, come, you big brute. Your head needs more purpose than an ear holder.* He ponders the problem and then announces openly to himself, "I need to go back to school."

Everyone in the Goon city goes on their usual daily business, while DuHero reads all the books he borrowed from the school. Many sunrises have passed since DuHero's amputation. His strength has returned but his pride is still hurting, as the feeling of incompleteness haunts his consciousness and the void in his undergarments. *I did not know I had other skills, such as reading, writing, critical thinking, and understanding many languages. The theoretical information is boring, but I love the practical application instructions.*

Over the course of the day, he learns dozens of new chants. Although his chanting capability is currently weak, he practices the chants over and over again to gain strength and conviction in his words. Flagrot's home fills with gases, damaged objects, light-emitting portals, and all sorts of random results through DuHero's continuous practice.

A call comes from outside. "Tabby is on a rampage again!"

DuHero hears the call but ignores any hint of concern. His subconscious reminds him to think about the message again.

Tabby.

DuHero puts down the book he is reading.

Tabby. What is a Tab—oh, Tabby! The Porc I killed at my first meeting with Goons. DuHero opens the heavy iron-studded door. *I want to see Tabby in action.*

DuHero hears commotion but can see no fighting. A Goon flies through the tree line and hits Flagrot's neighbor's house, head-first.

"Thank you for the directions, dying Goon," DuHero says to the face-smashed bloody Goon. "Impressive throwing distance," DuHero says to himself as a few more Goons fly over his head.

DuHero spots a crowd of creatures in combat; Tabby is the center of attention. As the mob tries to cut down Tabby, DuHero steps on a barrel near a food shop and hops onto the roof. He sits and watches Tabby crush skulls, maim limbs, eat ears, and catapult bodies across the sky.

"Very good, pig-man. You have a practiced and finessed fighting style," DuHero says to the air in front of him. "Oh, no. Not good, Tabby. I can see weaknesses I can exploit. I am glad the Goons are blind to your mistakes." DuHero leans over to his left side and rests his head on his pivoted arm. *Tabby is running out of Goons to kill.*

The last Goon is summarily stomped to death with Tabby's metal spike boots. Tabby pauses to catch his breath and turns, looking around for more action. Tabby is substantially covered in blood, wounds, and small lacerations. Seeing no more enemies to kill, Tabby promptly plops his body down in the mashed guts of a Goon, closes his large Porc eyes, and starts to meditate.

DuHero watches Tabby for a while. *My first time, I have a chance to study a Porc.* DuHero makes some observations. *Porcs are fairly large creatures, only slightly smaller than a Manbaby. Tabby has a pig-looking face with tusks curling outward from each corner of his mouth. His hands look nearly human, except the fingers are much larger, sharper, and thicker than my own. Hm-m-m, his weapons are a dagger that clings tightly along Tabby's right hip and a large mallet that lies beside him.*

"That battle was mildly entertaining," DuHero says as he stands and jumps off the roof to return to his studies.

"Do you not want to challenge me?" Tabby grumbles.

DuHero looks at the meditating Porc and speaks in a calm demeanor. "When you are at full strength, perhaps we can play."

"I do not play!" Tabby replies quickly.

DuHero is confused. "Then why did you kill all these Goons? I believe Goons would consider this minor massacre a typical, fun get-together."

"They provoked me. They know I go on killing sprees to relieve my tension."

"Do you feel better killing them?"

Tabby pauses to search his feelings. "No, not really."

DuHero looks at the Porc and smiles. "Tabby, I have no friends here. Would you like to be friends? Then we can play and do battles on our own terms."

"No one has ever asked to be a friend." Tabby stands, retrieves his weapon, and turns his back to DuHero. "I will think about it," Tabby says sadly.

"Sure, Tabby. Whenever you are ready. You know where I am staying?"

"Yes."

DuHero resumes his original course toward Flagrot's home.

"DuHero?"

DuHero stops to listen.

"Thank you," Tabby says, while whimpering slightly.

"That's what friends are for." DuHero turns and smiles. "Can I ask you something?"

Tabby faces DuHero and slowly walks to him, as each gushy step gurgles from his blood-filled boots. Tabby nods.

"Why are you named Tabby?"

"Goons give names to each other. The name helps me sell weapons and armor from my shop, due to my reputation."

"What is your reputation?" DuHero asks, to Tabby's surprise.

Tabby then remembers the circumstances of DuHero's existence in the land of Forever. DuHero is one of the few Goons with no memory of Tabby's rage. "I am called 'The Angry Blacksmith'—T. A. B. So, Tabby. I usually kill Goons with the weapons they end up purchasing."

DuHero's right eyebrow rises with interest. "Goons test their future weapons by receiving their lethal capacity?"

Tabby nods his head and is dumbfounded. "Goons claim they gain more stimulation and satisfaction with a kill when they know what it feels like to their victims. In a crazy way, their logic makes sense to the criminally insane."

DuHero looks into the Porc's bruised eyes. "So … your recent massacre is a sales convention along with an exercise regiment?"

Tabby returns the stare to DuHero's eyes. "I have the rare privilege of killing my customers to gain their sales." Tabby chuckles slightly. "I get to kill Goons, practice my fighting skills, and sell my custom weapons and armor. The more imaginative my slaughtering skills, the more sales I make."

Brilliant. This Porc fellow is truly brilliant. DuHero's thoughts are interrupted by a screaming Goon.

A man of fattish substance waddles at full slothful speed past Tabby's massacre scene. "The Snob Pink Sniper Knight killer crazy … help … ahhhhh! He is in the forest!" The Goon bends over to grasp his knees for a deep breath. Goons start to gather around the man. Tabby and DuHero promptly walk toward the congregation. The man continues. "In the forest—he was there on his white horse."

The Goons murmur with concern. DuHero tilts his head toward Tabby and whispers, "Could you tell me about this knight?"

"All right." Tabby pauses slightly to arrange his words. "The knight is an independent Snob soldier who has not realized that Forever War Three has ended. His purpose is to disrupt Goon supply convoys by stealth-attacking vulnerable Goons deep in our territory. No matter how much we yell to the knight to tell him the war is over, he continues to terrorize us."

DuHero finds this information fascinating, not only in the skill of the fighter but also the ironic word arrangement. "A war called 'forever' ended?"

Tabby picks up on DuHero's inexperience with historic events. "Forever is the name of this land all around us," Tabby says.

"Oh, yes. Flagrot briefly mentioned this during my multiple-death incident in the past."

Tabby grumbles and continues. "All the races have their own names, but they all roughly translate to 'Forever.'"

DuHero absorbs the information. "Tabby, would you like to join me to kill this knight?"

Tabby is a bit shocked but not surprised. "DuHero, hundreds of Goons tried to kill this man. He is quite an exceptional opponent."

"Good! I like a challenge. Tabby, grab what you need, and we will leave immediately."

Tabby looks DuHero over. "You have no gear or weapons. Let me see if I can find you something back at my shop."

"Thanks, Tabby. That would certainly help."

"You are also missing a dong," Tabby says in a droll tone.

DuHero laughs, frowns, and then cries in a matter of seconds. The Porc feels a hint of revenge as he remembers his last battle with DuHero. Tabby does not like to be bested in battle by Goons, especially by a naked one. His verbal thrust into DuHero's pride tore the man's soul as much as his pride. Insulted by Tabby's irreverence, DuHero turns to face him, wiping the tears away with his sleeve. DuHero uncomfortably asks, "Uhhh, Tabby. Do you sell ... well ... do you sell replacement dongs?"

Tabby quickly interrupts. "No. But you should wear protection next time."

"That improvisation from the Goon leader and Juulia was not part of the act," DuHero says in a defensive tone. "I call it a deeply judicial sacrifice."

"I call it judicial genius. Anything less and you would probably be in jail now."

Jail? That is right! I could have gone to jail. A hellish undertaking I luckily avoided. I suppose my sacrifice was necessary for my ignorance. "Thank you Tabby. I feel much better."

Although his observation was not intended to help DuHero, Tabby accepts the thanks by nodding his head slightly.

Armor and weapons gleam vibrantly as Tabby opens his shop

door and fills his shop with sunlight. Every wall, shelf, and ceiling has a tool of war awaiting blood use.

"Tabby, this place is fantastic. Did you make all this?"

Tabby nods as he wrestles free two swords, which are wedged blade-tip into the splintered wooden floor. DuHero is in awe. The wide variety of war equipment tempts DuHero to try every item at least once. He calms his excitement to think about their upcoming mission. "How does this Pink Knight kill Goons?"

Tabby hands a sword to DuHero, handle-first. He grabs the weapon with his left hand.

"Try this one," Tabby says with a small snort. He proceeds to answer DuHero's question. "The knight uses a variety of techniques. An arrow might suddenly hit a Goon in the skull. Sometimes the knight charges a convoy, unnoticed, and carves everyone up in the blink of an eye."

DuHero swings the sword with confidence. Feeling incomplete, DuHero grabs a small shield, clasps the strap tightly, and ties the shield to his left forearm. With his right hand, he snatches a larger-sized sword off the wall by the handle and proceeds to swing both swords in an elegant deadly dance. *My body knows what to do with these weapons but my brain is confused. Best to ignore the brain when slicing open necks.* He continues his dance of swinging swords, while describing his experience. *Yes, I understand, body. I can fight with two swords and a shield with ease. Do not use brain. I understand.* DuHero breaks from his inner consciousness to listen to Tabby's question.

"DuHero, do you know why he is called the Pink Knight?" Tabby asks.

"Tabby, I barely know how to put on my pants," DuHero says.

Tabby steps out of the backroom in black leather pants and shirt with no sleeves. The Porc has muscles stacked on muscles. His green arms bear the burden of faint tattoos that DuHero does not recognize. Tabby undresses a large stuffed dummy behind a counter. He removes the scuffed plate armor and dented helm. "Borrow anything you need, DuHero." Tabby fits on arm protection. "The Pink Knight wears pink armor."

DuHero, as usual, is confused at everything he learns. "He wears pink armor and rides a white horse. How can he remain unseen?"

"During the war, he blended into Goon ranks quite well. The uniform gave him lots of opportunities for sabotage. After a number of incidents, Goon military declared that no one was allowed to wear pink knight armor. The Pink Knight did not comply and instead changed tactics."

DuHero stops his dressing. *Fascinating. I would love to meet this man some day.* "Strange that he still wears the obvious armor. Any reason why?"

A clang of fallen shoulder armor fills the room. Tabby picks up the metal gear and places the scuffed protection on a counter. "I do not know. But he is brilliant at what he does. His capability to generate fear among Goons who handled logistics crippled our supply lines during the last war. He definitely hurt us in body and in mind."

"Why would Goons be scared?" DuHero asks.

"It is difficult to function without arms or legs. The Pink Knight trophy-chanted every Goon he could cut."

The two focus on completing their armor uniforms and weapons attire. As DuHero fulfills his weaponry needs, he asks Tabby, "Even if those Goons with missing limbs die and re-exist, do they still have missing limbs?"

"Correct," Tabby says.

So much for that idea to recover my missing body part. No matter. I have a plan. "We should travel light and bring some ranged weapons," DuHero says.

Shouting is heard outside. As DuHero opens the shop door, an average-sized Goon randomly yells that he has seen the Pink Knight. "I ran off, leaving my food cart behind," the troubled Goon says.

"Where can I find your cart?" DuHero asks, stepping outside

Tabby's shop. The Goon points down a narrow roadway as Tabby steps outside.

"I know where he is pointing," Tabby says. DuHero and Tabby gather what they need and begin their mission.

Abandoned on the road outside of the Goon village, between a forest and a field, a cart full of fruits and vegetables sits motionless. DuHero and Tabby approach the cart carefully, expecting an ambush. Tabby keeps his eyes on the forest close to the road and on the cart, while DuHero inspects the food. Some of the food has big bite marks, along with a few flies taking advantage of the exposed fruity flesh.

"Tabby, how good is the knight at killing Goons? Does he always maim them, or does he let some run away?"

Tabby keeps his attention on the forest. "In the past, he would kill everyone. After the war, he became sporadic in his killing. He must have learned that scaring Goons became nearly effortless when his solid reputation of being a terrorist completes the job."

Hoof prints are seen off the trail. DuHero inspects the tracks. "We should head that way," DuHero says while pointing toward the field. "The tracks lead across the grassy field and into that far forest."

"There is a small lake in that direction," Tabby says.

They leave the cart and follow the horse tracks. The walk is long. As they arrive at a lake, the area is clear of any man on a horse. "It's strange," DuHero remarks. "For a knight with the skills you described, he certainly isn't covering his tracks very well." They continue the slow pursuit but half the day has been spent, and the trail eventually ends on a stony landscape with miscellaneous forest patches. "We need a new approach," DuHero reluctantly admits. "This gear is flaghatingly heavy."

Over the next few days, no news of the knight surfaces. Tabby and DuHero meet once again at a Brewbarf, a Goon equivalent of a hovel with seats, tables, and spirits served by the barrel load. They discuss tactics, great battles, and the evil capabilities of bunny rabbits. Tabby hates bunnies ferociously, but he will not explain his reasoning, no matter how much DuHero pleads. After a few mugs of Goonbee Nectar, when the conversation becomes stale, Tabby asks about DuHero's friend Afffriend.

"Have you seen him in prison yet?" Tabby asks.

DuHero is venomous. "*What?*"

Tabby continues. "Re-education. That Manbaby cannot use the name you gave him."

"Goons are re-educating Afffriend because of me? In a prison? Why didn't you tell me this earlier, Tabby?"

Before Tabby can speak, DuHero stands quickly, knocking over his chair. Tabby leads them outside the Brewbarf, and then across the city to a large complex, which secures the undesirables of Goon society. DuHero sees a prison guard. "Can I speak with Afffriend please?" DuHero says.

"There is nobody by the name of Afffriend," the Goon prison guard says, without concern for verification.

"How many Manbabies are imprisoned?" Tabby asks with authoritative veneer.

"One hundred fifty-seven, many of them very recently," the guard jeers.

"May we see the Manbabies, please?" Tabby asks sincerely. The guard opens a door beside the main gate and pulls out two buckets filled with a foul-smelling pink substance.

"Treat me first," Tabby says, while turning his head away, trying to avoid the stink. A nostril plug is given to Tabby and DuHero. Tabby promptly slides it into his three-holed cylindrical nose and breathes in relief. Tabby receives the full treatment as the foul-smelling Pink Stink is poured over his head. DuHero gags as the stink assaults his senses to a magnificent degree. The guard quickly puts the nose device on DuHero. DuHero feels much better, as he also receives the Pink Stink shower.

The main prison gates open as a new prison guard pulls diligently on the metal, wood, and chant-resistant fortification.

"Why?" DuHero asks rhetorically. The pungent odor starts to seep through DuHero's nose device. DuHero snaps his wrist toward Tabby. A bit of stringy goo flies onto Tabby's face. The connecting pink goo forms a saggy spaghetti link between the two pink-covered creatures. Tabby brushes off the link and speaks while they are escorted through multiple locked doors and gates.

"We will be placed into the open prison population. For our safety, the treatment lets the prisoners know we are guests, and we will make them extremely sick if they get too close to us."

"Why do Goons seem to love pink so much?"

"I was told pink is the calmer color of blood-raging red." Tabby looks to DuHero, trying to catch his eye. "Goons ... well, many creatures need a point of focus to define themselves. The color pink brings mocking laughter to Goon enemies, especially with the bizarre and weak symbolism. Even my Porc brothers did not take any concern for Goons. But later, after Goons began dominating the last great war, nobody questioned pink dongs on pink flags, with a pink army wielding pink weapons. Pink became the new red."

Pink dongs. Sheesh, what foolishness. Funny, but hardly a call of greatness.

The last door opens, and prisoners watch the new arrivals.

"The Pink Stink also helps guards listen in on prisoner-visitor conversations. It will be difficult for us to get close to Afffriend, so we must yell our discussion."

Hundreds of prisoners fill the courtyard. Many self-segregate according to race and creature-type. DuHero sees a few creatures he has never witnessed before—a small, short group of green, smoothed-skin, anorexic creatures; a few entities that look like ground moles; others creatures that have a glowing aura of multi-colored resonance. DuHero wants to see more but a Manbaby notices DuHero walking into the center of the courtyard. The Manbaby becomes excited, drawing DuHero's attention. All of a sudden, many Manbabies hurry toward DuHero and form a perimeter around DuHero at a comfortable distance.

"I am looking for Afffriend!" DuHero yells over and over

again, with his hands cupped around his mouth. The Manbabies look at each other and mumble. A Manbaby squeezes his way through the crowd. DuHero sees Afffriend and smiles. "Afffriend! Good to see you."

Afffriend sits his big body down on the ground. His eyes start to tear, and soon other Manbabies follow his lead. DuHero is not sure if the tears of his giant friend are from the Pink Stink or a broken heart. "No, no, no more Afffriend. J-just Manbaby," Afffriend says as he sobs. A Manbaby behind Afffriend places his hand on the shoulder of his giant brother and weeps with him.

"To me, you will always be Afffriend. I do not care what others think," DuHero says with strong reassurance.

Afffriend smiles and walks to DuHero. Afffriend is able to grab a quick hug before he becomes unconscious from the Pink Stink. His fellow Manbabies drag Afffriend to his previous sitting position and slap his face a few times, trying to revive him. DuHero sits and waits while Tabby continues to stand at attention.

"Manbabies, this is Tabby! He is also my friend!" DuHero announces to the gathering while pointing to Tabby. The Manbabies murmur among themselves. Tabby sits next to DuHero, looking uneasy. Afffriend eventually recovers, sits up, crosses his legs, and looks at DuHero with happy sadness—a wonderfully ironic yet unusual combination of Manbaby emotions.

"Afffriend, I do not know how I can help you," DuHero says sadly. "All I can give you is advice."

DuHero pauses as the Manbabies lean in to listen. "Do what you want to do, and be what you want to be, Afffriend. Find your purpose in the land of Forever. Work with your Manbaby brothers to build all your dreams. I hope you understand what I am saying."

A Goon guard in the distance rolls his eyes with contempt. He pretends to barf, using gestures on his face; his fellow soldiers giggle.

"Organize yourselves to work together. Your brothers are your family." Many Manbabies begin sobbing. Tabby cannot believe what he is witnessing—an army of powerful strong Manbabies holding each other and profusely crying. A Goon guard with the rank of Skullcracker sees the commotion and instructs DuHero and Tabby to leave.

DuHero stands. "Everyone, hold your noses, please!" DuHero walks over to Afffriend and hugs him. "Be strong and brave, Afffriend."

The Manbabies clear a path to the gate. DuHero and Tabby leave the prison and find the nearest lake. They thoroughly clean themselves.

Word has spread throughout the city that the Pink Knight is ambushing more food carts at the southern outskirts of the city. Goons gather in a field just outside Pink Bosom to watch as the Pink Knight allows his horse feed on the spoils of another abandoned food cart. Everyone keeps a safe distance, as more and more Goons gather, wielding an assortment of crude weapons. The Goon leader Refailable arrives and prepares his appearance for negotiating terms. He straightens his armor, wipes his face, and brushes any loose ends of dangling meat from his scruffy beard.

DuHero, Juulia, and Flagrot arrive. Everyone watches the knight intensely, expecting a huge confrontation to take place. Refailable steps out of the crowd.

"Honorable knight, I am Refailable, Goon leader of all Goon territory. I wish to inform you that the war ended long ago. Your kingdom is awaiting your return."

The Pink Knight remains motionless. The horse continues to munch on vegetables.

"Honorable knight, you are a great warrior, and we respect your capabilities to do us harm. If you wish to stay with us, we can give you land and peace, if you so desire." Because the knight wears a solid helmet, there is no facial expression for Refailable to analyze. "We can build a home to your liking." There is no response. The horse plops a souvenir of fertilized food on the ground. "All right. A mansion with farm animals and slaves." The horse moves a bit and continues to stuff its mouth. "Would you like a territory to rule? I can give you that. Gold, coins, resources, Jargoons—anything you want."

Flagrot steps into Refailable's view. A smirk lines Flagrot's tired face. "Why don't you give him all of Goon land, the stars, and your stained undergarments?"

Goons snicker at the remark as Flagrot gleams a retarded smile. Refailable looks cross but does not flinch at the criticism. He knows Flagrot always seeks to insult authority at opportune moments.

"I am quite competent to handle this situation. After all, I am an expert in diplomacy."

Flagrot holds his tongue and thinks, *Anyone who claims competence, isn't; calls himself an expert is definitely not; and declares self-sanity usually is not.*

DuHero walks slowly toward the Pink Knight. Everyone watches but says nothing. The Pink Knight takes no notice, but the horse stops eating and watches the approaching man. DuHero continues his slow pace, and still the Pink Knight shows no concern of his approach. Closer and closer he moves; no reaction. The horse sniffs the air and seems to be docile. Quickly grabbing the reins, DuHero struggles with the horse as it stands on its rear legs. The horse lifts DuHero; the large beast jumping in the air. The Pink Knight appears ready for attack while the crowd cheers. DuHero struggles to gain control but after a few more horse jumps, the Pink Knight falls onto DuHero, and both lose the grasp of the horse reins. A wrestling match ensues, and the Pink Knight chokes DuHero with a forearm covered in heavy armor. DuHero punches at the Pink Knight's mask; the mask starts to come off. A petrified eyeball falls out of the mask and lands in DuHero's gasping mouth. DuHero shifts his weight, and the Pink Knight slumps to his side. DuHero laughs as he coughs and spits the unwanted dead eyeball from his throat. The horse sees the unusual shriveled treat and gobbles down the blue eye. DuHero pulls off the mask fully to see a rotting skull lazily mono-staring to the right. The horse runs off as the crowd gathers around DuHero, and Flagrot inspects the body.

"This isn't the knight. He probably took a Goon body, dressed it up, and secured it to the horse. Smart deception."

DuHero sits up, wearing a goofy grin. "He is probably back in Snob land, swinging his dong at the ladies while we run around like scared little girls."

The crowd enjoys the comment. Refailable orders the body to be buried immediately. Refailable looks at DuHero with smugness and walks away. Juulia is uncomfortably impressed with DuHero's antics.

Later that evening, a party is held in DuHero's honor at the nearest Brewbarf.

Chapter 7
Exploration

"How goes the search, Pool Keeper?" Queen Ovulum bellows as she sits in her throne. All the queen's servants feel uneasy, knowing the queen might erupt into uncontrollable anger. The time between the discovery of the World Pools containing the queen's son and the present has been filled with frustration and unachievable expectations. The pool keeper and the queen have met numerous times, and the result usually brings projected items to the man's skull. This time he wears a hardened black dome to protect his head.

Pool Keeper Jacqueustow Clum, Kingdom Liaison for Pool Supervising Activity, looks damp as he gives off a pond stench, which is difficult for the court audience to ignore. He holds up a parchment to read a rehearsed report. "My queen, we sent down twenty-five professional searchers into the Questionable World Pool."

The queen interjects, "Must you call the World Pool 'questionable'?"

Before the elderly man can reply, a glass cup crashes against the left side of his head.

"Servant! Too soon," the queen says, as if scolding a naughty child. "When I give clear indication of my disapproval of his answer, I will signal you."

The servant re-arms himself with more breakable objects. "My apologies, my queen," the servant says, and he bows for forgiveness. "His presence alone seems to give you displeasure."

Jacqueustow grimaces while the queen stares at the slightly troubled pool keeper.

"Yes. Yes, he has. Regardless, please give him a chance to talk."

The servant nods in agreement. The queen smirks at Jacqueustow. "As you can see, old man, I contracted my physical reactionary displeasure to random servants in my courtroom."

Jacqueustow turns his head slightly to find the other object-throwers. He shrugs off any further concern and returns to his parchment. "My queen, we sent down twenty-five professional searchers into the ..." He pauses to find a better name for the pool. "Into the Q World Pool."

Many in the courtroom take a relaxing breath. Jacqueustow continues. "Three died on arrival, five continually changed into horrific mutations—now we can't find them, nor do we know what they look like—and the rest turned into ..." He pauses to wipe the sweat from his chin. "The rest turned into bunny rabbits."

"What are bunny rabbits?" the queen says.

"Small furry animals with big ears, lots of speed, and—"

The queen interrupts. "Claws? Weapons? Search skills to find my son?"

Without a moment of delay, Jacqueustow gives his answer. "Their primary skills seem to be having sex, eating their dung balls, and making more bunnies."

Servants giggle as the queen droops her head. She signals with her right hand, and several breakable objects land on the reinforced head of Jacqueustow. Once the noise of shattering crystal subsides, the queen speaks. "Can any of these creature-servants help me find my son?"

Jacqueustow brushes bits of broken pottery off his shoulders. "Well, yes. Yet the desire for sex keeps distracting them from their mission."

The Ministerial Science Advisor to the Queen, named Beeker DeHawn, walks toward the queen and whispers in her ear. The queen waves him off. "You may ask your questions, Minister." A servant hurls a vase at Jacqueustow, misinterpreting the queen's signal. Jacqueustow dodges the projectile, which promptly finds the face of a prominent religious representative. His underling guides the bloody-faced man out of the courtroom.

The minister speaks with clarity and without regard to the damaging incident. "Pool Keeper, have you determined why our people turn into random creatures in the Questionable World Pool?"

"No," the world pool keeper regretfully answers.

"Have our kingdom's servants, now bunny rabbits, reproduced in the land of Questionable?"

"Yes."

"How many bunny rabbit servants do we have in the land of Questionable?"

"We stopped counting after 53,000."

Everyone's eyes widen and murmurs are heard throughout the courtroom. The queen stands and screams, "Find my son! Do anything to find my son!"

Jacqueustow runs out of the courtroom as dozens of objects crash-rain on him.

*   *   *

"Please, I beg you, return my dong to me," DuHero whines as he leans over Flagrot's table.

"Dong? Oh, your psin," Juulia replies with hurtful delight. She leans on the table with one arm and diligently beams her smiling delight into DuHero's gazing face.

"Psin? Is that the same as dong and diagonal protrusion?" DuHero asks.

"I suppose, foolish man. Every culture has a name for that male weakness."

DuHero leans in a little closer. "You are truly enjoying this with your happy-hurt grin."

"Of course I love seeing you suffer. Nymphs thrive on watching others suffer for pleasure—happy-hurt, as you comically call it."

DuHero needs something to fight back. "I see your mother died pushing those enormous hips through her baby passage."

Juulia is shocked. "You copious discharge of a diseased snake. I—" Juulia is interrupted by an old man's surly tongue.

"Thank you for the entertainment, children! Let us remember that I am older and wiser than the words you share, so each of your insults needs work." Flagrot walks to Juulia from the next room and places drinks on the table in front of her. DuHero and Juulia stare ferociously at each other. As Flagrot sits on the most convenient chair at the table, he unrolls a map, ignoring their silent staring war. "I believe our destination is here." Flagrot presses firmly in the near-center of the map. Both DuHero and Juulia break their visual duel to study the diagram.

"That is near the center of neutral territory. Are you sure it is there?" she queries with true concern in her voice.

"Reasonably sure," Flagrot mumbles as he swigs his bitter drink.

"What about Boortards?" she asks.

"There is no denying that we may run into them. We will be prepared," Flagrot replies.

"If this is dangerous, should we have more in our party?" DuHero says.

"I want to keep this small. Who did you have in mind?" Flagrot says.

DuHero promptly answers. "I only know Tabby. He is quite capable, and he is my friend."

"Heh. Unusual choice, but this journey is something he may

enjoy. Yes, he can come. Juulia, can you think of anyone else we need?"

"I cannot."

Flagrot gives them details of their departure. The table clears, and DuHero heads to Tabby's store.

$$* \qquad * \qquad *$$

Pigfeeler, a self-proclaimed pupil of Flagrot, watches from a distance as the early morning gathering of Juulia, Flagrot, DuHero, and Tabby stand in front of Flagrot's home. Pigfeeler heard of the group's gathering through his spy activities the day earlier. He tries to listen in as the group discusses small details of their future adventure, while reviewing their gear and fitting their armor. With no such luck, Pigfeeler stands and stares at the private gathering within the shadows of the morning sunrise. The party begins to walk down a quiet road; Pigfeeler follows.

Once the group leaves the boundary of the city, DuHero quickens his pace to walk side by side with Juulia. "Juulia," DuHero says as Juulia gives him dirty looks. "I am asking you politely one more time. Please, can I have my body part back?" She ignores him. The quick pace, leveraged by well-maintained Goon rock roads, makes the trophy dangle melodically with each step. DuHero becomes slightly depressed, eyeing the morbid trophy, his symbol of manhood, flailing in obscurity on her belt. "I am concerned for your safety. My dong is cursed."

Flagrot raises an eyebrow in curiosity, while Juulia smirks. Tabby does not listen, as his thoughts focus on designing his own private, secret life plan.

"If you give me the trophy and release it from your chant, you should be fine," DuHero says.

"Shut the hole in your face, weak man," Juulia says. "I will not be fooled by your foolishness, you fool of fools."

DuHero slows his pace, falling behind the group.

They walk for half the day with no sign of the mysterious

curse or any indication of Boortards. Juulia does feel a bit strange. Something pokes her lightly around her body but not enough for her to be concerned. "Excuse me. I need to be alone." Juulia places her gear immediately on the ground next to the roadway and rushes to the nearest thick bush.

"We might want to rest here. Do your business. Eeeaagh, my back," Flagrot says with a groan as he carefully places his back bag on the ground next to Juulia's gear. Flagrot starts some small-talk. "Tabby, what made you decide to join us?"

Without hesitation, he replies, "To help a friend."

DuHero smiles as Flagrot makes no physical sign of slight suspicion. Flagrot knows Tabby has other goals than helping a friend.

As long as that Porc's ambitions do not conflict with my own agenda, we may end up helping one another. Maybe kill one another. No, his motives are usually noble. His assistance has helped my cause for a while now.

Juulia's condition becomes worse. Over the last two sunrises, she has stopped the party forty-seven times to find a bush to expel her insides. She has had random chills, cramps, and one time blew out the contents of her nose uncontrollably on Flagrot's back. On the third day, she is in tears. Her body swells in random places. She once again runs into nearby bushes, and the three men wait yet again for her return. Juulia screams. The men drop their gear and prepare their weapons. She runs out of the bushes toward the men. She stops in front of DuHero, whose sword is slightly turned away from cutting the nearly nude nymph. She tears DuHero's dong off her belt. The small rope snaps, and she throws the trophy to the ground, making a faint thunk on the well-walked pathway. She proceeds to whisper angrily the chant to release the body part. "MiNa EnAm EiHoOlI OmA SuReJa SaAgIsT!"

She then proceeds to stomp relentlessly with her boots on DuHero's ex-trophy-chanted body part. The men are mesmerized by her bobbing cleavage as she pulverizes the body part with her blade-decor black boots. She suddenly turns and returns to the bushes.

"Flagrot, what happens to my dong now?" DuHero asks. His emotions are mixed when he sees the flattened flesh.

"It should appear back to normal at any time."

DuHero sticks the end of his sword into the earth and pulls at the waist of his pants and undergarments. "Ahhh. Hello, old friend." He lets go of his pants and retrieves his weapon.

Tabby leans in to consult DuHero. "How did you place the curse?" he whispers.

DuHero whispers back, "There is no curse. I used a bunch of kid's magic chants to drive her crazy."

Tabby becomes more curious and wants more details. "The times she felt cold?"

"A chant called Create Wind. Just enough to make her feel cold in places."

"The cramping and swelling?"

"Create Water chant focused inside her body."

Tabby is awestruck at DuHero's trickery. "The frequent bush stops?"

"Create Water in her bladder."

"The recent screaming?"

"Transfer Objects into her butt. Her last bush stop had spiders and centipedes."

Tabby, for the first time in a long while, is shocked. He cannot speak.

DuHero continues. "For the last three days she has expelled numerous objects."

Tabby tries to hold back his laughter. He drops his Grand Hammer to cover his mouth with both hands.

DuHero continues. "I started with berries, sugar cubes, and nuts and then moved to stones, small carrots, and even small children's toys."

Tabby's eyes water. He suddenly bursts out laughing so hard that the noise startles nearby animals. Birds vacate the trees swiftly.

Flagrot smiles as he watches Tabby roll on the ground, holding his belly and laughing until he loses breath. Tabby recovers from his belly laugh after a fair amount of sunlight noticeably changes the shadows. Juulia continues to stay in the bushes while Flagrot and DuHero sit casually on a grassy patch just off the hard dirt path.

"You know about the Goon following us, Flagrot?" DuHero asks nonchalantly to avoid turning curious heads.

"Yes. He is an idiot who wants to learn my chants and understand my inventions."

"Should we kill him?" Tabby says, while trying to spot the unwelcomed Goon.

Flagrot points to the direction in front of them. "We need to take care of that Boortard first." From the distance, a Boortard watches the group of three. The normal-looking man-creature makes no threatening gestures.

"That is a Boortard?" DuHero says with little concern. "He is dressed like a regular soldier for an army of unremarkable fighters."

Before the creature can grab the sword strapped on his waist, six arrows whiz through the air to pierce his head. Before the body can fall to the ground, Juulia sprints to the Boortard and places five daggers into the dead chest. DuHero is erotically shocked as Juulia chops some trophies and recovers her daggers. She casually walks back to the bushes to redress. DuHero asks innocently, "Flagrot, how come women do not have dongs?"

After a lengthy day of walking, the group of four turns off the main path toward a spectacularly tall mountain.

"We are deep into neutral territory. Be on the lookout for all sorts of creatures, traps, distractions, and graveyards," Flagrot says with a blunt, cautious tone. "Let me lead."

"What if we die? How will we find each other?" DuHero says.

"I usually call out using a unique scream so my sisters can call back, and then I follow their voices," Juulia says.

Tabby speaks. "That may attract more attention than we can handle. Graveyard Boortard Gravers could be present and continually kill you hundreds of times."

"Gravers? You mean Boortards live at a graveyard, killing creatures continually for no reason?" DuHero asks.

"There is a reason, DuHero," Flagrot says. "We cannot understand the purpose. Just simple blood-thirsty savages, is my guess. No honor."

"We have many troubles with Gravers in Porc territory," Tabby adds.

"Sometimes Boortards try this in Nymph territory. My sisters patrol the graveyards to prevent such a travesty."

"DuHero, if you recover in a graveyard stacked with thousands of bodies, try to hide or run away as fast as possible," Flagrot says. "That graveyard is camped with those Graver fools."

"Understood."

Another day passes. Except for a few violent animals trying to attack the party and failing, the journey is relatively quiet. They reach the bottom of the mountain, and Flagrot is convinced there is a hidden path in the near vicinity. The foliage, rockslides, overgrown moss, and fungus make the mountainside appear decorated and alive. The group knows a mountain exists in front of them, but after a certain point, the forest around the mountain seems to deliberately hide physical orientation, along with sunlight in some places. After a strenuous search through the unusual camouflage of shrubbery, Tabby finds a worn yet dominant path inward, after hacking through a thick patch of Spiral Thorn bushes. After carefully gauging the path created by Tabby, Juulia hands Tabby a damp cloth so he can clean the hundreds of cuts on his arm. He accepts the cloth, only to wipe the sweat off the smooth, short, brown, hairy forehead.

"Stand back, everyone!" Flagrot says as he lifts his hands toward the barely useable thorn path. After a few moments of silence, Flagrot says loudly, "Tabby, Juulia, did you hear me?"

Tabby relays back with the same tone, "We are far inside away from the bush."

With a few intense syllables, Flagrot directs the chant of an extremely cold and vaporous wind through the entire thorn bush. His chant ends, and the thorn bushes become frozen solid, with tiny gleaming icicles dangling off most of the thorns.

"Fall before me!" Flagrot yells brazenly at the delicate foliage. Nothing happens.

In the distance, Tabby calls out, "What?"

"Fall before me, great barrier of death thorns!" Flagrot says to the bush.

Tabby yells once again, "What do you mean by 'death thorns'?"

DuHero turns his head to Flagrot, with one eyebrow raised, noting his confusion with the unnecessary orders to the frozen plant.

Flagrot is irked. "Fall you cur ..." Flagrot hurriedly walks through the pile of neutralized thorn bush. The weight of his body makes many thorns crack, groan, and then collapse to the ground in a silent yet prominent crash of straining brittle branches. Flagrot and DuHero can see Juulia and Tabby in the distance, beyond the dusty ice pile of thorns. Before anyone can question Flagrot's unusual orders, Flagrot raises his left hand, signaling silence. Flagrot walks through the entire expanse of neutralized thorn bush. DuHero follows Flagrot and studies the scope of damage done to the area.

"Flagrot, I am always impressed with the power of your chants. You must have destroyed fifty paces deep of that strange bush."

"That particular chant freezes an area so cold, everything within it falls to iciclictic dust." DuHero can sense that Flagrot uses big words to magnify his moderate abilities. DuHero ponders. *I wish my worn utterances projected the same zeal and tenacitsies ... tenac ... ten ... darnfarnit, I hate that "ten" word.*

DuHero runs to one side of the destruction and then counts foot paces to the other side. "Amazing. Twenty-six paces," DuHero says as he looks upward to the tops of surviving shrubbery. "I guess … hm … fifteen paces high. Flagrot, have you tested the limit of your chant powers?" DuHero asks.

"To some extent. Yes."

"Is there a limit to chants?"

"No, not that I know of. But at my level of experience, some chants seem to improve only slightly. I always need more chants, more power, more effectiveness. That quest never stops for me."

Flagrot and DuHero saunter to Juulia and Tabby. She has cleaned most of Tabby's wounds. The group looks at their surroundings with some achievement.

"We are inside the mountain," Juulia says as her voice echoes in the far distance.

"Let us walk," Flagrot says. The group slowly trots inward down the large gullet of the mountain access. Each footstep clomps, while every word muttered echoes with repeated dominance.

"Interesting," Flagrot says while eyeing the details of his surroundings. "This path is well lit yet no light source is seen. The stone floor is well worn with scarring, probably caused by large equipment."

Every step they take is sloped downward and turns slightly to the left. The path spirals downward, never expanding or narrowing. No obstacles or even rubble interrupts their journey.

"I have hiked through caves and tunnels. This is not a normal cave," Tabby says after their second day of trudging in the mountain.

"What is a normal cave?" DuHero asks.

"Randomness. Pathways expand and shrink and break off into all directions. Dampness, fungus, and moss grow near water pools; animal hair and bones and feces litter the area," Tabby says as he raises his right hand to feel the wall. "The rock is fairly consistent. No impurities, no real sharp edges, no changes in color. It's been smoothed down."

"What about those holes along the ceiling?"

Everyone looks at DuHero's hand pointing to the well-lit

ceiling ahead. The farther they walk down the spiral path, the more they see hundreds of random-sized openings lining the wall, no bigger than a mouse hole, not big enough to fit through unless one is a mouse.

"Stop. Everyone!" Juulia warns with a feminine yet stern voice. Everyone stops and remains motionless. "I sensed traps when we entered this cave long ago. I am feeling something similar now."

DuHero becomes irate. "You did not warn us before."

Juulia keeps looking around the cave walls with caution. "I was hoping you would step on a trap so I could identify the danger."

"And watch me die," DuHero says.

"Of course," Juulia says.

DuHero notices a small wooden ball held in place by random bits of rubble. He reaches for the out-of-place object, rolls the small ball onto his thumb, and holds the sphere by his index finger. He flicks the ball, hitting Juulia in the left check. She blinks with surprise and smirks at the gesture. Both feel victory with their current tacit duel.

Tick-tick-tick sounds can be heard behind the group. A few small wooden balls roll by the group, downward along the spiral path. More ticks and more balls roll by the puzzled group. The ticking becomes indistinguishable from the sound of heavy rainfall hitting a thin metal roof. Hundreds of balls roll around their feet, like a river.

"DuHero!" Juulia yells with utter contempt.

"Do not blame me!" DuHero says. "I only retrieved one ball."

The flow of balls becomes shin-high, then knee-high, then waist-high. Flagrot begins to keel over, losing his footing. "Everyone, secure yourselves," Flagrot says, trying to maintain an upward balance. Tabby removes his belt blade and tries to pick into the rock. Juulia adjusts her footing, only to fall and be swept down the cave.

"Juulia!" DuHero screams like a panicky girl.

Flagrot chants Body Magnet. Everyone suddenly feels a shove, and they unwillingly join together, except for Juulia, who struggles against the ball flow. The flow increases in intensity. Juulia is soon covered with moving balls. Only a bump of balls at Juulia's position indicates her presence, like water smoothly rushing over a shallow boulder.

"DuHero! I will cut you … *again!*" she prominently says. The ticking sounds turn into a low rumble, as tens of thousands of tiny misfit balls run past. The torrent rises higher. Higher. Higher.

Flagrot chants the Body Magnet children's verse over and over again, struggling to keep them in place. Minute after minute, the flow intensifies.

"Go with the flow!" Tabby says with determination. "We … we cannot keep fighting a river."

"Under—*ugh!*" Flagrot tries to reply but a wooden ball fills the gap in his mouth with perfect proportion, wedging the foreign object tightly. The group flows downward. DuHero catches Juulia, and the group lets the river pull them down the cave.

"Hold onto each other, and try to grasp the walls and the ground to slow our descent," Tabby says. He notices Flagrot is choking. A quick punch to the chanter's stomach quickly releases the wedged object from Flagrot's tongue. Flagrot lets go of his grip of Tabby. Tabby expects a sudden release and secures Flagrot to the group by biting Flagrot's garments as he ties his waist with a rope. The entire group is now connected by a rope. Everyone tries to grip the cave walls, ceiling, and floor the best they can. They carefully continue their descent downward. After an hour, the volume of the entire cave is covered with moving balls. The rushing balls create a steady stagnant rumble.

"My arms are tired and scraped bloody!" DuHero says.

"So are mine!" Juulia replies.

They cannot see each other through the balls but the occasional rope tug reminds them they are still a group. "I am thinking about this trap!" Flagrot says.

"I as well!" Juulia adds. "A trap usually has a purpose! This I cannot phantom any reasoning!"

"What do moving rivers have?" DuHero asks. The group is puzzled with the question but then understands and summarizes that DuHero's mind is like a Manbaby, but he smells better.

DuHero cannot notice the sympathetic faces his colleagues are making beyond the balls. DuHero repeats the question louder. "I feel we are trapped in a rushing river. Besides drowning, how do people die in circumstances like this?"

"Broken bones by hitting boulders," Tabby says.

Juulia speaks soon after. "Fear and panic. I know some of my sisters die from emotional breakdown due to stressful conditions."

"The path seems clear of obstacles, and we are coping rather well," DuHero says as he focuses his thoughts to his bloodied arms. "What about being scraped to death?" DuHero says.

"Waterfalls! Rivers usually have waterfalls!" Flagrot says. "The sound of the rushing balls has changed! Hold on to the ground or wall; we need to get out of the flow now!"

As each of them tries to stop his movement, DuHero jumps upward slightly to reach the roof. His palms flatten, and his boots toe into the stone. "I see it! I see the falls!" DuHero screams with certainty. "I also see another passage! Move to the left and hug the wall! You should be able to escape the ball torrent!"

Each member of the party crawls to the ball-flow edge. DuHero is the first to find the diverse passage not inundated with balls. Tabby soon follows. Flagrot signals to DuHero that he will chant Magnet Body. Tabby and Flagrot are able to grab the cracks and ridges in the walls and resist the magnet.

"MaGnEt BoDy," Flagrot says at a frantic pace. Juulia and Flagrot drag quickly through the flow to Tabby and DuHero. Everyone escapes the rapids.

Their skin and clothes are multiply scratched, torn, and polished. Any exposed skin is coated red, brown, and gray. The wood, walls, and blood have changed the attire and attitude of the party.

"Our equipment is gone," DuHero says as he checks his weapon. "Good, my sword remains."

Everyone else instinctively reaches for his primary weapon.

Juulia pats herself around her waist. "Trophies. Many are gone," she sadly says. Her quick temper focuses her words toward DuHero.

"Before you burn your tongue on DuHero's existence once again, turn around," Flagrot says, while looking past her shoulder. He continues, "There is a room ahead. Let us explore that direction and then maybe your thoughts of potential regret may flow away like the trap we escaped."

DuHero stares intently at Flagrot. *Oh, you cunning man, Flagrot. I wish I massaged the language half as well. Juulia will not fall to your wordy charm.*

Everyone recovers and begins a short walk to the room ahead. As they approach, the room's vastness reveals itself.

Flagrot stares in amazement. "Incredible. The enormity of this lit chamber is amazing." Strewn on the ground are thousands of objects, mostly covered in dust. As they walk farther into the brightly lit expanse of the designed chamber, they notice a monolithic door in the distance. The garbage lying about changes to complex machinery as they move closer. Powerful war machines lay destroyed. Bones, armor, and weapons are bent, snapped, or scarred. A huge grave pile of creature casualties lay strewn all over the base of the Great Door. In different states of decay, the broken equipment shows war-like intention against the giant barricade of a perceived doorway. The gleaming wooden door is polished waxy burgundy, untouched, and ready for the next assault. They walk closer, turning to gaze at the occasional rotting skull, wince at the bloated stench of animals, and look at the door's architecture, which to their eyes screams for attention. Glowing, encrusted jewels promote their presence to the room, and golden statuettes covered in superb garments cling to the door, some with eyes and smirking faces, mocking their next contenders. The Great Door emanates everything that appeals to newcomers.

Flagrot gazes upward. He calculates in his mind that the door measures thirty DuHeros high, fifty DuHeros across. Many symbols engraved on the door show intertwined double spirals connected by horizontal bars. They remind DuHero of the ladder he climbed in the past.

These door ladders are twisted, much like my Goon sentence hearing.

DuHero notices a strange scent in the air. "Do you smell that?" DuHero says, then takes another deep sniff.

Juulia takes in a deep cache of air through her nose. She sniffs once again, closing her eyes and smiling. "I know this—what? This cannot be," Juulia says.

Flagrot snorts. Chunks of phlegm slide into his throat. He spits the sticky contents at a mutilated shield near his feet. He takes a deep breath. "I can breathe." DuHero looks at Flagrot with puzzlement. "Whatever is in the air is clearing my insides and making me feel young again," Flagrot says as he takes another deep breath.

Juulia sniffs again. "Barfolimin stew. Why can I smell Barfolimin stew? It was my favorite dish as a child. But only one person I know can make it smell this good." She pauses. "She lives in the Nymph village of Sensxexua. She cannot make this stew here. It requires fresh ingredients and cooking tools only found in her loft. She can barely walk, so as kids, we needed to be at her home to receive the wonderful broth."

DuHero introduces his version of his experience. "Dolphin brains covered in boar spine marrow dashed with cemetery stone fungus." He pauses to think about what he just said. *Why do I know that? Why do I want to kill someone in order to taste that dish? I wonder what a dolphin is supposed to be?*

DuHero becomes distracted by something shiny in the distance. He points to the desirable weapon attached to the lower left side of the door. "Look at that weapon! I want it!"

Juulia has her gaze on a beautiful multi-shot crossbow sitting on a shelf attached to the door. Flagrot walks closer to DuHero and Juulia while observing the door. "I see temptation, too." Flagrot points to the location of sparkling potion bottles, old books, and assorted items. "That cabinet fixed on the upper door contains everything I want."

"What is this place called? The Great Door of Temptation?" DuHero asks.

"Why does a door garnish so much temptation? I wonder if that is truly a door," Tabby says, while trying not to look at his material desire of a female dress, a perfect erotic fit for his wife.

"The large horizontal handle on the right side of the door dictates the difference. Maybe the door only allows a very large creature to open it," Flagrot says.

Regardless of the insight, everyone in the party still has the urge to pillage their independent discoveries from the welcoming yet mysteriously formidable door.

"Pigfeeler, you can join us!" Flagrot yells as the chamber echoes his voice. The group looks away from the door, trying to see the follower. Flagrot calls out once again.

"It appears your shadow will not accept your invitation," DuHero says to Flagrot.

"The Great Door has a chant book that could teach you tremendous power. Come see it," Flagrot says with welcoming assurance. Behind a scarred barricade in the distance, a small man stands and deliberately shows himself. Pigfeeler wears a chanter robe he stole from a ceremonial grave of an old dead lady. He walks toward Flagrot. Flagrot points to an area on the door within his throwing distance. "Why don't you find a stone so you can knock the book down from the shelf?"

Pigfeeler looks around his feet and finds a small piece of torn metal; he picks it up, walks to the door slowly, and raises his arm. The metal shard completely misses the book and hits the door. A massive spark flings the metal across the room, hitting the ground near the cavern's entrance.

"That was spectacular," DuHero says.

"Keep trying, Pigfeeler," Flagrot says calmly. The party, one by one, independently takes cover behind objects that can shield them from some danger. Tabby kneels down behind a damaged cannon shield. Flagrot steps behind the working arm of a catapult, which surprisingly is still in good shape. Juulia and DuHero sit behind piles of garbage, while keeping one eye at Pigfeeler's attempt to satisfy his greed. Pigfeeler throws an assortment of small objects he can find. Each time, the object leaves the door at high speed, singed, burned, or disintegrated.

Flagrot attempts to analyze the situation. *This door must have an energy source beyond anything we know in the land of Forever. With proper input, we could extract large amounts of output. This journey is already paying off. Harnessing this power would accelerate my long-term plans for the domination of the land of Forever.*

Pigfeeler throws a really weak volley and barely grazes the door. The door's reaction flicks the object back close to Pigfeeler's feet.

Aha, that is interesting. The force is reactionary with a multiplier of pressure. If Pigfeeler were to touch the door, one finger of pressure would output a hundred times of pressure back, breaking and burning his finger. "Try to climb to it, Pigfeeler. I think you can use the strange ladder on the left to reach your book."

Pigfeeler ignores his words and turns his attention to Juulia. He ogles her cleavage as she stands and walks to the door, inspecting potential weaknesses.

Soon everyone loses interest in Pigfeeler. Tabby finds his interest in the smashed equipment around him. "So many powerful machines destroyed. I do not see how we can go any farther," Tabby says to Flagrot as he walks toward him. "Looks like all our races attempted to penetrate the door at one time in history."

"Good observation, Tabby," Flagrot says. *Tabby continues to impress me.*

"This is like a huge sub-standard museum of Forever's past. I could learn a lot from studying this equipment and integrate past ideas into my modern weapon-making. I hope to come back soon, provided the ball river does not kill me," Tabby says.

"To conquer a river, bring a boat," Flagrot says.

"That would probably get me killed. The objective is to go with the flow, but don't let it consume you."

So much for keeping Tabby away from this place. I think I will need to make a deal with him before the knowledge of this place becomes known and the next battles begin.

Before Flagrot can impose any partnership, Pigfeeler causes a distraction to ensure future drama. "You are hot," Pigfeeler coos at Juulia. He approaches her and slaps her butt and tries to run for the chamber exit. DuHero intercepts the little pervert as Juulia arms herself with a dagger and a star-like spikeball. DuHero approaches Juulia with the wrangling Pigfeeler dangling in his right hand.

"Juulia, I am sorry we fought in the past," DuHero says calmly. Juulia is surprised and drawn to DuHero's honesty. "I do not want us to fight anymore. As a gift, I give you this scrawny runt for your murderous pleasure."

Juulia is stunned and confused. She takes the gesture as an honest one, while her heart starts to beat faster. DuHero waits patiently, wearing a smile, while Pigfeeler squirms and tries to free himself. Juulia smiles and turns her attention to Pigfeeler. Flagrot speaks out to make a suggestion. Everyone agrees to the proposal. After Juulia takes a finger trophy, DuHero loads Pigfeeler on a large projectile device facing the door. Before Pigfeeler can escape the contraption, Tabby releases the tension of the throwing device, flinging Pigfeeler toward the door. The door unceremoniously— but spectacularly—blows Pigfeeler to pieces. Burning body parts fly all around the room.

DuHero gnaws on Pigfeeler's cooked leg as the group sits around a campfire, surrounded by the ancient and dilapidated bones of past camps. Flagrot is engulfed by intense thought as he studies the door. Juulia sneaks random peeks at DuHero. DuHero notices, smiles, and offers the half-eaten leg to her. She politely refuses. He waves the leg but no one demonstrates interest. He returns to his morbid meal.

"A bit of news from home, DuHero. You know the Pink Knight's horse? The one carrying the dead body wearing pink armor?" Flagrot says.

DuHero nods.

"Goons were trying to catch the horse, and they stumbled on to the Pink Knight's trophy-chanted cache of Goon body parts. Your heroism has made a lot of Goons happy again with their reacquainted appendages."

"I certainly know how that feels. That's great to hear," DuHero says and takes a huge celebratory bite of Pigfeeler flesh. Juulia keeps her gaze away from DuHero.

"Wait. How can they release the chant? Did they find the real Pink Knight?" DuHero says.

"There are costly ways to recover the flesh. It helps that the original trophy-chanted part is recovered along with the owner. Someday, I will explain the process to you."

DuHero shrugs his shoulders and continues to devour the large meal.

"Do you know cannibalism is frowned upon in Forever?" Juulia says.

"My stomach—mmmmfm—doesn't care," DuHero says as bits of meat spray from his mouth.

"Yes. It certainly doesn't," Flagrot says with observed caution. Although there is no indication of sunlight or moonlight within the enclosed chamber, everyone knows they all need rest. Flagrot is determined to know how to open the door, but he too falls asleep.

Tabby awakes, startled. He shakes the snow covering his head. *Those dreams were way too good to be true.* Tabby notices the campsite scenery has changed. Flagrot was sleep-chanting during the rest period. To keep himself occupied while he waited for the others to waken, Tabby counted the new things at the campsite from unconscious chanting.

Five frogs, one poisonous snake, seventeen spoons, forty-one ... no, forty-two decks of playing cards, two badgers chasing six geese, eleven rubber mallets, a flock of pigeons circling the room above our heads, and twenty-four piles of what I truly hope are piles of brown pudding. Oh, I must not forget the small snowstorm that lightly blankets the area.

Tabby reaches over and extinguishes the small fire on his boot.

And the random boot fire. Flagrot, you are too dangerous when you sleep.

The minor firefight wakes Flagrot. As he gazes around the vicinity, he is not surprised at the strange objects at the camp.

Squeeeeeeak!

"Flagenfarns!" Flagrot curses as he reaches deep into his nose to pull out a children's whistle toy, a device that identified itself by Flagrot's nasal breathing. He throws the toy at DuHero but misses. The noise wakes Juulia. Her eyes widen as she turns her head to DuHero. The erotic dream she experienced fills her mind with doubt and surprise. Her subconscious has teased her with images of potential futures, many of which include DuHero in compromising sexual positions. She quickly dismisses these options.

DuHero is sleeping on his left side, snoring and facing away from the group. He mumbles a few words. A small pile of oatmeal slop falls from the sky and hits Tabby on the head. Tabby kicks at DuHero slightly. He kicks again, and when DuHero rolls onto his back, the group gasps at the unexpected scene. Flagrot rolls his eyes, Tabby laughs, and Juulia blushes as she tries to look away from DuHero's diagonal protrusion, which is at full mast within his pants. Tabby gives DuHero a good hard kick. "Wake up, you erect fool," Tabby laughs and kicks again.

"Again, I smell my favorite morning meal," Juulia says with a somber groan. The others sniff the air with delight. The door stares at the group with temptation. Everyone tries to resist the urge to make a foolish attempt at acquiring their material pride. Tabby bends his head downward in tearful shame. He smells the meal his partner would cook for him when he lived in Porc territory. He stands, starts yelling random words, and pulls out his hammer.

DuHero quickly stands and holds Tabby in place. "*No!* Don't do it, Tabby. We need you alive," DuHero sympathetically yells.

Tabby continues to scream while tears roll down his face. "It is not fair! That door … that door is reviving my past! That evil thing needs to die!" Tabby tries to out-wrestle DuHero but fails. Juulia joins Tabby with the crying, while Flagrot looks downward with sympathy at the pitiful struggle. Tabby shrugs DuHero off his person. Tabby's hammer hits the ground, as Tabby turns away from the door and walks to a sheared, slightly burnt log, and sits. The group joins Tabby, each taking a comfortable stance to stare at the problem. They stare intently, believing an event or positive solution will unravel before them. The plan is not working.

"Look at us. We are mesmerized by all this temptation," DuHero says, pausing to sniff the air. "Not only does it give us eye and nose temptation, it tells us that it is a door. A door tells us there could be more fantastic temptations behind it. The monolithic size magnifies the infinite possibilities of complete happiness and power. Well, that is how I see it."

Juulia is surprised at DuHero's insight. She turns her head to Flagrot. "Is this what we came for, Flagrot? The door?"

"No. I do not believe this door is the end. There must be something else, something even more."

Tabby covers his face, thinking of Flagrot's words. *Even more? This man sees no limits to possibilities. I envy his youthful unrestricted imagination, or I dislike his madman outlook. I am not sure which character plays the role.*

"I do not understand. How can you claim there is something more?" DuHero says.

"The door wants our concentration, like an attention-seeking whore Goon. What a distraction," Tabby says.

"Good, Tabby. You are thinking similar conclusions as I," Flagrot says.

DuHero closes his eyes and sighs, knowing a long, boring insight of knowledge will fill his ears.

"Those with vain, pride, ambitions, greed, and selfishness will be blinded by the immense potential offering. The door screams 'Take me if you can. I dare you to try!' When failure multiplies, then more is thrown at the problem. The worst damage is the destroyed reputations, shattered dreams, the ego of desire that falls apart, breaking even the strongest souls."

"In simpler terms, those who want it the most have the most to lose," DuHero surprisingly summarizes, even shocking himself.

"Hmphrp," Flagrot grunts.

Juulia stands to look around. "The rest of this chamber seems barren. I wonder if the true entrance is hidden somewhere in those desolate walls."

Flagrot goes to Juulia. "Yes. That could be it. The walls are multi-shaded gray. Perfect for camouflaged doors, switches, or paths. Everyone, go to a wall and follow your hand along it. I will check the pathway into this room."

"I found something!" Tabby yells, cupping his mouth with his hands. After a full day of searching, every member in the party is glad to hear something positive. Tabby points to a place in the wall that looks open at a certain angle. The area is blocked by a makeshift shack, one of hundreds scattered around the chamber and partially destroyed. Everyone begins dismantling the obstacles, piece by piece. DuHero tests a few of his chants to move the larger objects. He discovers he can only move small scraps of wood, but he knows the chant will grow stronger with practice and better pronunciation. Flagrot uses the same chant to remove a large roof pillar and flings the heavy object into the distance. DuHero is in awe of the smirking Flagrot. DuHero uses all his energy and voice to match Flagrot's skill. The target of his chant aggression changes into boiling tar and promptly catches fire. Flagrot tries to extinguish the flame but cannot, no matter how much water is chanted. Frustratingly, he throws the infinite flaming blob into a remote area of the chamber. After all the debris is removed, the pathway still cannot be easily seen, due to blending gray patterns. They have to run their hands across the wall and find it is bent inward and into a passageway.

Flagrot lights the pathway to see that it leads deep downward into the mountain. "Brilliant. We are correct. The Great Door is nothing but a huge distraction," Flagrot remarks.

Everyone is excited and cheering. As the party moves into the corridor, Flagrot chants, and a large stone in the distance floats toward his position. The object rests gently in front of the passageway. The jagged black stone does not block the passage but provides enough coverage to keep others from accidently discovering their find. Another chant blows the air to cover any tracks or indication of their recent presence.

After spending a day running from an outside graveyard to the great door, Pigfeeler hears the strange winds and darts into the chamber toward the door. "The door is closed," Pigfeeler says and sighs to himself. Pigfeeler falls to his knees in despair as he knows he's lost his opportunity for greatness, due to his indiscretion with Juulia. He stands and walks to the door to embrace his fate.

Chapter 8
Bunny Numbers

Refailable has just released another flaming arrow that penetrates the skull of a bunny rabbit. A Goon messenger encounters the entourage, and Refailable's guards caution the messenger to approach carefully.

"What is it, Messenger?" Refailable asks as he ties a bag filled with explosive powder onto a bunny held by his servant.

"Dear leader, all of the Manbabies left Goon territory. We do not know where they are," the messenger says.

Refailable grabs the bunny and flings the white furry animal down a small escarpment into a colony of "busy" bunnies. Just as the bunny lands, Refailable flames his arrow, aims, and then releases. In a matter of seconds, a nest of bunnies turn into a mess of bunny body parts. The entourage laughs.

"Find a Manbaby and interrogate him," Refailable says.

"Dear leader, there are no Manbabies anywhere."

"What? Those moronic creatures gone? Were they kidnapped?"

"Dear leader, no, we believe they all left voluntarily. Even the Manbabies in prison are gone."

Refailable ties two bags onto another bunny. This time he

adds a cord to one bag and lights the dangling end. "Did they use chants to escape?"

The fuse-lit bunny rabbit is thrown into another crowd of bunnies. The thrown bunny scampers into a hole, and a rushing puff of dust is seen shortly after.

"Dear leader, no, they broke out during the night, and we only noticed the hole in the wall in the morning."

A servant holds a rabbit in his hands; Refailable gives him a signal. The servant moves and kicks the bunny upward; the damaged bunny falls down the escarpment. Refailable successfully hits the airborne target as the bunny lands with a dead thump.

"Who helped them?" Refailable says with some reservation.

"Dear leader, we believe they organized and planned the escape themselves."

Refailable looks at the messenger for the first time as he loads bunnies into a basket attached to a projectile device. "Manbabies, organized? That's like saying 'dry water' or 'Goon intelligence.'" Refailable looks to his entourage. "Boost the power of the mini-CATapult with your chants." As the group primes the mini-CATapult, Refailable walks to the messenger. "Tell me ... how did they escape?"

"Dear leader—"

"Enough with the 'dear leader.' Just tell me."

"Uh, yes, de—" The messenger shakes as the imposing Goon leader looks down at him menacingly. "Sir, the Goons are calling it the Thoomp Escape Dance."

Refailable continues staring at the messenger, expecting more detail.

"The ... the Manbabies inside and outside the prison gathered and started jumping up and down in unison. When they landed together, it made a *thoomp* sound. They did this for half the day yesterday. What is strange is that prison guards on the walls were telling me the Manbabies inside the prison were jumping in the same rhythm as the Manbabies on the outside. Over five hundred Manbabies were doing the dance together."

Refailable sees a bunny trying to climb out of the basket. He rushes over and gently pushes the bunny back in. "How does jumping in one spot cause a hole in the prison wall?"

"We believe they sat down and kicked the wall with the balls of their feet. When the Manbabies landed, they kicked. That's why we didn't hear them, and they blocked the wall with their bodies so we didn't see their dedicated wall-kickers."

Refailable adds, "And the Manbabies on the outside distracted the guards, believing there would be an attack on the prison."

"Yes, de—" The messenger stops. "Uh … yes."

"So there are no Manbabies anywhere?"

"No. Goons are complaining. The Manbabies handled many laborious tasks for them."

"Meh. Manbabies are not slaves, even though we treated them as such. Thank you for the message, Messenger. As a punishment, tell the prison guards they need to wear the Pink Stink every day this week. And have them fix the hole in the wall."

The messenger memorizes the instructions and heads back to the city.

"*Pull!*" Refailable yells with surprising exuberance. The bunnies from the mini-CATapult fly high into the sky, slowly spreading apart. They then start to descend and disappear from sight. Tiny thumps can be heard in the far distance. "Well, so much for returning the bunnies to the fluffy clouds."

The entourage laughs at Refailable's comment. Refailable thinks to himself, *I wonder why so many bunnies are appearing in Goon kingdom.*

*   *   *

After visiting another graveyard, Pigfeeler's conclusion to his future is to grace his presence in the local taverns to swill his problems away. Uncountable days later, Pigfeeler unknowingly finds himself at another tavern in another neutral village. He's lost track of who he was, where he was, and what his purpose was in Forever. Drink after drink feeds his internal painful loss with temporary numbness. Tavern patrons grow tired of his slurred stories of the Great Door and how he is going to avenge those individuals who left him behind. Nobody knows of DuHero, Juulia, Flagrot, or Tabby, but their names are cursed often by the one-man hate machine.

Many sunrises and taverns later, Pigfeeler finds himself drinking in Snob territory. He can tell, as the patrons are dressed very well, even for peasants. The tavern drinks have snobby names, such as Rouge Wine, Sunset Ale, and P.P. de Cheval Apple Cider. He tries to keep his composure, as he is a Goon, and Snobs do not take kindly to his type. But after his fourth drink of Fleurmerde plant juice, his mind releases his defenses, and his Goon attitude comes out. He steps on his chair and proceeds to recite his practiced rant about the Great Door and its power. Most patrons find his antics amusing, and they allow the drunken jester to continue. Pigfeeler tries to mock the party members, but all he can do is focus on DuHero. After dropping his pants and trying to imitate DuHero's diagonal protrusion, he is promptly thrown out of the tavern. His madness reaches a new level of spontaneity. He finds a thin rope, ties one end to himself and the other to the tavern. As he tries to walk away, he openly declares himself to be a king and that the tavern is now his servant. The tavern building refuses to give in to his demands. As he tries to pull the tavern away once again, he falls asleep, standing but leaning slightly forward, as the rope and tavern hold him up.

The next morning, he finds himself lying in a field with dozens of ropes tied to his body. He does not feel restricted as he stands. Still woozy, he tries to maintain his balance, but his feet are tangled in the ropes. He lifts one arm, and the ropes tied to it pull a teddy bear and a mop lying in the grass. As he walks forward, he can see he is dragging a number of random objects. Included in his collection is an unpolished skull, beer mugs, a baby rattle, a dead cat, a book called *Failed Relationships: The Revenge Guide*, and other objects he cannot identify. His mind is trying to work out what happened. Suddenly, he remembers. The objects are his entourage, and he, as King of Objectionism, demanded his servants to follow him. He wanders back to the village with his kingdom dragging behind him.

The town is in chaos, as half the buildings have burned to the ground. Townsfolk run back and forth to the well, trying to extinguish any flames still hungering for fuel. Some women cry; men hold their heads in disbelief as the once-beautiful wooden and stone dwellings, which sheltered many Crazyrage season provisions, have been destroyed. The dirt road is littered with buckets, half-burned blankets, and soiled rags that wiped away soot. Many townsfolk are still in shock, yet fully capable of expressing their anger. The rants become louder as Pigfeeler enters the main meeting area of the town. Pigfeeler's existence becomes the focus of their revenge or justice. The crowd becomes a mob of ranting anger.

A townsman points to Pigfeeler and speaks loudly. "It's him! I saw him on my neighbor's rooftop, dancing and crying out for love. He then jumped down and started urinating in the town well and said, 'What's yellow and smells like pee? Yourrrrr boots!' and the fool turned around and wet my foot."

Another townsperson rants, "I know this person. Yesterday at the butcher, he kissed a live pig and then my eldest daughter and yelled, 'This pig is wearing lipstick!'"

Pigfeeler raises a small smile but no one in the crowd returns it with his own. A Snob dressed in red authoritative-looking clothing makes his way through the crowd. "Were you the one who drew that very long image on the ground in the middle of the village?"

Pigfeeler thinks back into his drunken past, then remembers. "You mean the image of two round circles and a long dong attached to it?"

"Yes," the authority replies.

Pigfeeler smirks. "No."

Pigfeeler lands face-first onto the hardened floor of the local prison. His object entourage fails to follow.

*   *   *

"Only follow me. I sense traps on some of these paths. Stay close to me," Juulia warns.

"Yes, I can sense the chanted portions of these hazards," Flagrot adds.

Juulia's superior tracking skills help the party navigate through the maze of halls, small empty rooms, and long pathways. A few times, they go in circles, but everyone is still confident of Juulia's scouting skills. DuHero is impressed by how Juulia can find useful, safe paths, as he can see no indication of direction or danger. The corridors become larger the deeper they travel. Juulia suddenly stops. DuHero was not paying attention and accidently bumps into Juulia.

"Whoops, sorry. My fault," DuHero whispers as he checks Juulia to confirm she is not hurt.

Juulia has an angry look, but her expression changes to kindness and a little smile. Tabby notices their eyes and smiles. He knows the two have a destiny in the near future, provided they do not kill each other too much.

"There are strange noises ahead," Juulia whispers. Nobody else can hear sounds of whooshing clanks, but Juulia pulls off her crossbow and slowly walks ahead, as if danger is close. Everyone else slowly prepares their weapons.

The noise gets louder and audible to the rest of the group. Eventually, they reach a large cavern filled with unusual equipment, strange pictures flashing on the walls, and miscellaneous tables and chairs scattered about.

Flagrot's eyes water with emotion. "This is it. I can't believe it exists." He tries to read the symbols on the walls, but they change too fast for him to translate. As they walk into the heart of the chamber, they see round panels on the floor. No one has seen machines or architecture of this kind before, all of which draw their curiosity. Flagrot notices a smaller static display of numbers on one of the machines. He walks over and tries to analyze the puzzling symbols. Everyone puts their weapons away and watches the flashing pictures of Porcs, Snobs, Goons, Nymphs, and unusual, unknown creatures. DuHero wanders around and steps on one of the platforms. A huge image of DuHero appears on the wall. Tabby notices the image and points up. "Look at that big Flaggot," Tabby jests.

Everyone turns, and DuHero is shocked to see a big image of himself, replicating his every movement. DuHero waves; the image waves instantly. Again and again, he moves his body, and the image moves with synchronized accuracy. He draws his sword, and the big image does the same.

Flagrot's mouth opens wide. He is shocked beyond any experience in his known life. Flagrot walks over to a different platform and steps on the circle. A huge image of him appears beside DuHero, along with dozens of symbols. Tabby and Juulia follow, and four huge images of the party fill the wall.

"Please stay in the circles. I need to study the symbols," Flagrot says.

Everyone continually stares at their own images. DuHero notices that Tabby stands on a platform beside him. DuHero steps closer and punches Tabby hard in the shoulder. "That's for calling me a Flaggot."

Tabby smiles as he tries to rub his painful shoulder through the leather armor. A punch like that represents true friendship to Tabby.

"Do it again," Flagrot demands.

"Do what?" DuHero asks.

"Punch Tabby," Flagrot says.

Tabby and DuHero exchange glances of agreement and DuHero punches Tabby in the same place.

"Excellent. Now Tabby, punch Du—"

Tabby is well prepared and punches DuHero hard in the face

before Flagrot can finish his sentence. DuHero stumbles back in shock, but he smiles at the painful gesture.

"Their symbols have changed," Juulia says.

"Yes. Punch each other a few more times," Flagrot says. "But stay in your designated circles."

The two exchange blows like regular fighters, except they do not guard against damage. They actually enjoy the battle. Flagrot pulls out a parchment and begins scribbling furiously with his finger.

"Yes, yes. You two can stop now," Flagrot says quickly as he continues using his ink-flowing chanted finger to add information he's witnessed. "Juulia, please walk over to DuHero."

She complies.

"Juulia, cut off DuHero's fingers, please," Flagrot asks nicely.

Normally, she would not hesitate, but in this case she really does not want to harm DuHero.

DuHero holds out his right hand. "Go ahead, Juulia, I do not mind. It is to help Flagrot."

She again hesitates, but then she grabs a sheathed chest blade and instantly removes two fingers from DuHero's hand. DuHero is in deep pain. She tries to apologize but she cannot speak. She turns away, runs, and cries behind a sophisticated-looking box of levers, buttons, and small lights.

"Fascinating. So that's how it works," Flagrot says as he admires the carnage on the wall. DuHero's wall image showers blood, and ancient symbols appear to describe the incident, displaying numbers and illustrating external hues that focus around the wound. Data scrolls away from the wall as new information appears. Flagrot knows what the large display represents, but he remains silent in his findings.

Tabby picks up a severed finger and pretends to begin a trophy-chant. DuHero tries to grab the finger with his injured hand, only just realizing he is missing his fingers. He uses his other hand to grab the finger, while Tabby laughs.

Many hours pass, and DuHero's injured hand is back to normal. Juulia is still out of sight, Flagrot continues to study the monitor near the platforms, and DuHero and Tabby sit in their respective circular platforms.

"Flagrot, how long do we sit here?" DuHero demands.

"You can step off the platform. I have enough information to get started," Flagrot says as he yawns.

Tabby and DuHero walk over to Flagrot. He quickly demonstrates his mastery of the device, which shows random creature images and lots of strange symbols.

"There are creatures somewhere on our planet that we haven't seen. See here," Flagrot says, while pressing a few buttons on a panel. The men study the unusual creature on the wall screen, formerly occupied by their self-portraits. DuHero sees a hideous six-armed monster, with polished, dark plates for skin and a face full of extending teeth.

"A new type of Boortard?" DuHero asks softly.

"Let us hope not. That thing is geared naturally for battle," Tabby says.

Juulia quietly walks to the men, gazing up at the image of the unknown creature. She composes herself as if nothing happened in the past. "Flagrot, could you explain to us what we discovered?" Juulia asks politely.

"What we see is something I will study for thousands of suns," Flagrot says.

"But what is it?"

"That creature is called ... ill ... Ilkasoo—no, an Ilkasu." Flagrot points to the left of the monitor. "Those symbols you see are numbers. These special numbers represent the Ilkasu and everything around his environment. From what I studied in early folklore, these numbers represent our entire existence. They called these numbers Digitals. Digitals are the micro-building blocks of you, me, that chair, everything!" He pauses to catch his breath. He points to some symbols near DuHero's image, which suddenly re-appear on the wall. "Those symbols are meta-representations of other Digital combinations that make up DuHero. Blocks of Digitals can be represented as other Digitals."

DuHero tries to grasp this knowledge, but he goes back to staring at Juulia's beautiful eyes.

"So what am I?" Juulia asks cautiously, not really wanting to hear the answer.

"You are a unique design of an array of Digital clusters. The world around you has its own set of unique Digital arrays. As we interact, our Digital array clusters change."

"Array?" Juulia wearily asks.

"A big block of numbers of Digitals is an array. I am having trouble distinguishing between numbers and Digitals. They can look the same, but how they react in the meta-array of existence is a big mystery."

Juulia is puzzled but comes to grips with the new knowledge. "What do we call these building blocks of our existence?" Juulia asks.

Flagrot ponders for a long time. Tabby grows tired and looks around for something comfortable to sleep on. Tabby finds his resting place and walks away. DuHero follows and then Juulia. Flagrot does not notice his party has left him to solve Juulia's question alone. Not far from Flagrot are dozens of beds and three sleeping, familiar creatures.

"A Digital Numbers Array—that's what we are!" Flagrot screams in a whisper, enjoying his eureka moment. Juulia wakes to find Flagrot looming over her bed. "We can call it Digital Numbers Array—DNA for short," Flagrot whispers with intense excitement. Juulia is uncomfortable with how close Flagrot leans toward her. He moves his mouth close to her ear. "If I can learn more about DNA, I can possibly fix your problem. But it will take time."

Juulia feels safer upon hearing that sentence. Her face displays exuberant optimism. "Thank you, Flagrot. You are a true friend to my Nymph sisters," she whispers into Flagrot's ear.

Flagrot still stays close. He wants to say more. "Juulia, I can see you have feelings for DuHero." Juulia blushes and looks at DuHero, who is comfortably slumped in his cot. "I believe he will be a good man for you in the future." Flagrot leans in even closer. "Invite him to Nympholymphus so both of you can learn more about the other."

Juulia turns her head quickly. "But my sisters!" she whispers loudly.

"Yes, I know. It will be a challenge, but you must trust me," Flagrot says with insistence and moves to hold her right hand.

Juulia rises from her cot. She grabs Flagrot's sleeve, pulls him away from the sleeping Goons, and finds an area of the chamber for privacy. "What if he says no?" Juulia demands.

"He won't. I believe he likes you, too. He is like a lost boy, trying to understand this world. Be patient with him." Juulia is truly scared. Flagrot now holds both her hands. "Most importantly, you must feed his ego. Men thrive on women recognizing their need to feel manly and useful. Do not forget this."

Juulia is not sure exactly what he means, but she knows his advice is serious. She nods in agreement.

"I will announce that I won't need help anymore and everyone can go home. At this time, please ask DuHero to escort you to Nymph territory," Flagrot says.

She nods positively once again.

He smiles and chivalrously kisses the top of her left hand.

While Flagrot and Juulia are talking, Tabby and DuHero have their own conversation.

"Listen, you Flaggot," Tabby says seriously. "Juulia likes you, and I know you like her. If you want to be closer to her, give her the 'little things.'"

"You mean children's toys in her butt?"

Tabby smacks DuHero in the head. "Be serious. Women thrive on lots of little things that make them feel happy. Give her a flower, a caress of her arm, a compliment on how beautiful she looks. The more you give her, the more she will want to be with you."

"But I don't know what that means!" DuHero whispers loudly.

"Another hint: Listen to what she says, but don't try to solve her problems unless she specifically wants solutions."

"Huh?"

"When a woman wants to talk, let her talk. Acknowledge that you are listening by waving your head, saying 'I see,' holding her hands, or smiling when she needs a smile."

"Over here, everyone!" Flagrot calls out.

"Remember what I said," Tabby says with insistence.

As the group gathers, DuHero and Juulia exchange shy glances.

"Thank you, everyone, for escorting me here. I will be staying to study this magnificent invention. Juulia, please say hello to your queen for me. DuHero, I am sorry we didn't spark your memories to discover your origins. I am hoping this device may give us clues to help you."

"Thanks, Flagrot. I enjoyed my travels with this group," DuHero says with a smile.

"Tabby, could I speak to you in private? You two talk," Flagrot says as he pushes Juulia slightly closer to DuHero.

As Tabby and Flagrot walk to another part of the cavern, Juulia has trouble making eye contact with DuHero. "DuHero. Uhhh … DuHero, could you escort me back to Nymph territory?"

"Aieeuhuhh, yes. Yes, I will help. But why? You are quite capable of defending yourself."

"Uhh …" Juulia is trying to be honest but she needs another truth to cover her fondness for his company. "I need a man such as you to protect me in case we confront Boortards," Juulia says and sighs with relief.

"Yes. Yes, I can protect you." DuHero pauses to think of what Tabby said about flattering a female. "I would love to see your blades slice the throats of Boortards and you cut off their dongs." *I hope my compliment worked.*

Juulia has a look of confusion, but she understands the message and thinks to herself, *Not perfectly romantic, but I will take it as a good attempt.*

Flagrot and Tabby are deep in discussion. "I will follow your instructions, but I will need lots of resources," Tabby says.

"Yes. I will get what you need in the future. Do the best you can for now," Flagrot says.

Everyone says their good-byes and leaves the chamber, except Flagrot. He sits down at a smooth white table and gazes lovingly at the devices surrounding him. He looks at the task around him. *My mind wants to be nourished by the stars. I am imprisoned, observing the universal performance above my head, trapped on a tiny blue bead floating in the tide of potential. This tears the fabric of my sane existence. Until now. Now, at least, I may have found my amorous employ. Nothing contributes so much to stimulate the mind as a steady purpose and unquestionable love.*

Chapter 9
Plots of the Powerful

Refailable slumps down into his throne recliner. His leaders sit comfortably at the table close to him. "All right, you Flaggots. What is on the agenda today?" Refailable says as he leans back with his arms behind his head.

The Minister of Miscellaneous Flaggotry, a position responsible for stimulating and regulating the cultural activity of Goons, speaks. "Aside from the usual Flaggotry, there are a few items that may be nothing. But in the future, it could turn into something important."

"Great. Tell me about the Flaggotry," says Refailable.

"Nothing new. Goons urinating in drinking cups; Goons playing 'catch the axe with your face' disputes; petty thefts; graffiti; and one case of unauthorized donkey races through the city."

"Who won?"

"A Goon named Micker Schlub."

"Penalty?"

"He has to clean his donkey with his tongue."

"Good. Glad to hear our Goon judicial system works. Next."

"First item of real business: the Manbaby search. There is no trace of Manbabies, and Goons have stopped caring to search."

"Stop searching. May Goonocracy thrive." Refailable closes his eyes, pretending to sleep.

"Next topic," the Minister of Miscellaneous Flaggotry says. "We have reports of cats and rabbits attacking each other."

Refailable laughs hard, holding his large belly and expelling some gas. "Continue," he says as the air fills with the stench of sour milk.

"Dear leader—"

"Enough! I am tired of that old Goonexicon. If anyone utters that phrase in my presence, they get a warning first. Second offense, they get jailed for the day. May Goonocracy thrive."

The notes taker hastily adds the new decree to the empirical records.

The Minister of Miscellaneous Flaggotry starts again. "We have found thousands of dead bunnies and cats throughout the kingdom. Witnesses have seen bunnies with explosives running to a clowder of cats and detonating themselves, killing everything in the area."

The Minister of Trade and Greed, a position of importance that deals in resources, money, and anything valuable, speaks. "Are you sure it isn't just Goons fooling around?"

"Yes. Witnesses have seen bunnies tying the explosives to themselves. No Goons were involved."

The leaders look dumbfounded.

"Who would teach bunnies to tie explosives to themselves?" says the Minister of Wrecking Stuff, a position of least importance, as no official war happened to need his service.

Refailable starts to whistle and thinks to himself, *Smart little horny Flaggots.* He speaks harshly. "Why do we care?"

The Minister of Miscellaneous Flaggotry replies, "Cats are an important part of our military arsenal. If they keep dying, they may leave us like the Manbabies."

The room falls silent for a minute.

"What can we do to help our cat brothers?" Refailable asks with slight contempt.

The Minister of Wrecking Stuff speaks proudly. "Arm them with modified claws, flame-ball spitters, tail blades, and spike helms. Most cats are trained to use these weapons we invented for them."

The Minister of Trade and Greed contributes, "A bunny-killing Goon festival. Goons can kill them for entertainment, food and fur. But to make this a reality, our Dear ... uh, Refailable needs to set an example so his cult following will copy his actions."

"What does this mean? What do I need to do?" Refailable asks.

"Make a statement. No, not just a statement—make a fashion statement. Wear bunny fur, participate in the hunts using fur-laced weapons, be at the rabbit feasts, and use bunny fur to wipe your mouth."

Refailable holds both hands to his face. "Ugh. I can just imagine what Goons would do. Those Flaggots of ours would make dung-ball soup or wear rabbit-fur underwear and bunny-ear nipple tassels."

The group laughs as the Minister of Miscellaneous Flaggotry speaks. "It has been a while since we've done anything Goony at a kingdom scale. With Goons everywhere wiping out rabbits, we could keep both Goons and rabbits under control."

"Fine. If we are all in agreement, say dongs."

The entire group yells "Dongs!"

"All right. The bunny-bashing festival is a go. May Goonocracy thrive."

*   *   *

The queen of Ovulum is exhausted. The constant worry of finding her baby boy interferes with her sleep and judgment. "World Pool Keeper, what is the status of the search?" she wearily asks.

"My queen, the war is hampering our efforts to—"

"*War?* What *war?* Who authorized a war without my

permission?" she shrieks as she grabs a bowl of raisins and throws the contents at the keeper. "Keeper, War Minister, follow me."

The three move into the queen's war chamber. The room is decorated along the walls with armaments from past achievements. The large, boisterous table of blue crystal creaks and cracks from overuse as the queen leans over and slumps down into a chair. "I am sorry for my outbreak, Keeper." She starts weeping. The keeper kneels to hand her a mess cloth he keeps handy for the many vegetable stains he receives from Her Highness' projectile anger. The war minister has never seen the queen in this emotional state. He becomes quite uncomfortable as the mess cloth becomes soaked with additional tears. "Keeper, please continue with your report."

The keeper sits in a crystal chair next to the queen, while the war minister chooses a seat away from the queen in an unconscious sign of distancing himself.

"My queen, our bunny-rabbit servant population is growing out of control. Creatures that hunt us bunnies are starting to take notice as our numbers grow. To focus the bunnies on our objectives and to manage the threat, we looked to cats as a possible enemy."

"Possible? You mean you instigated the war?" the queen asks.

"War was going to happen. Cats and bunnies do not cooperate, so we began our attacks immediately."

"I haven't seen what a bunny looks like. Do we have the capacity to wage a war?"

"Once we were able to communicate and invent devices to support a bunny's unique flaws and characteristics, our war armies became quite successful."

"Flaws? Like what?" the queen asks.

The war minister shows little interest in the discussion. He twirls a cone-shaped button on his blue ceremonial robe. "Rabbits cannot use their voices, as compared to human speech. But with superior rabbit hearing, rabbits can pick out the inflection and enunciating attempts of bunny-pronounced words, which are similar to human sounds, and we now can communicate clearly. We also invented a device to give active opposable thumbs to our rabbit army. With this device, we can imitate human hands and grasp almost anything. We even have reports of bunnies swinging through trees and climbing mountains."

The queen stares intently at the war minister. Her eyes tell the message to him that he should show interest in the conversation. The war minister pretends to cough and interjects, "Um. Hrmf. What is the status of the war?"

"Why do you know so little about this war, War Minister?" the queen asks scornfully.

"No one told me," the war minister boisterously answers.

The keeper responds quickly. "We tried many times! The Exploration Society was told by the war minister that the war was an 'exploration' matter. He then says it was out of his jurisdiction and that it didn't use any troops under his control."

"I said no such thing!" the war minister arrogantly lies.

"The arrogance of your responses tells me you did," the queen responds with a verbal throat-cut to his lie. The war minister's eyes shift left and right, rapidly looking for a positive answer to break the tension.

The keeper tries to steer the conversation back to the problem. "At first, we were doing quite well. Our pre-emptive strike on their cat cave left their leadership trapped inside while we destroyed the entrance. Bunny war parties would attack and kill solo cats, while our Boom Bunny Special Forces detonated themselves near groups of cats."

"So how did the war change?" the war minister asks.

"Two major problems. A group calling themselves 'Goons' are killing us in great numbers. We do not have the capability to fight these giants."

"They are giant?"

"To a rabbit, yes. Goons are mostly like you or me in size. The second problem is that cats re-exist when they die."

The queen and the war minister turn their heads to look at the keeper. The keeper notices and continues with a bit more confidence. "When a cat dies, the same cat appears at a graveyard. We believe it is the same exact cat with memory of its death."

"A graveyard produces life?" the queen asks.

"I am not sure about new life. But pre-existing life, yes."

The queen's mind races with thoughts of justification for the search. Her people do not have this re-existing capability. If she could find and control this power, she will not need the boy-king to inherit her power when she dies. She would just re-exist and reclaim her throne.

"My queen, re-existence would be an extremely valuable tool for our military," says the war minister with excitement in his eyes. "It would give us an understanding of the steps toward death under different circumstances. Once we die, we can re-exist and document our discovery. Incredible. It would be like immortality with mortal experience."

"Does every creature in the Questionable world have this re-existing gift?" asks the queen.

"Yes, except us. When a bunny servant dies, it is permanent."

"My queen, I recommend we call off this war," the war minister insists.

"Yes, I understand. The fighting needs to stop. We need to change our focus to a reconnaissance plan. I still want to find my son."

"The Science Inventors Society has developed a device to recognize Ovulum entities. Residents from our kingdom, and their offspring, can be easily distinguished from Questionable world creatures," the keeper says.

"How?" asks the queen.

"When you point the device at one of us, we glow and give off a colorful aura. This works on fellow rabbits."

"Excellent!" the queen exuberates. "Since my baby came from here, he would glow."

"Correct. No matter what type of creature he became, we can detect him."

The queen immediately looks healthier, and her eyes have lost the dead look of hopelessness. "War Minister, I want you to go to Questionable and lead operations to find my son and discover the secret of re-existence."

The war minister is shocked. "Me? But I could die!"

The queen is a bit shocked at his reaction.

"My queen, I like war but I do not want to die for it," moans the war minister.

*   *   *

Flagrot steps outside into the sunshine. He looks around the area to make sure no witnesses are present around the entrance to the Great Door. He looks up at the mountain, focuses, mumbles, and a small chunk of the mountain explodes above the Great Door path. The path is now secured by a pile of rubble blocking easy entry but not completely enclosed. He walks along the mountainside and repeats his chants. All along the mountainside he creates rockslides, rock traps, and waterfalls; he replants bushes, trees, and fields of grass. He continues his landscaping all around the area, and he even tries to move portions of the mountain to no avail. He finds a graveyard that has piles of thousands of rotting corpses. Using another chant, corpses start to fly, one by one, into the direction of the Great Door path. When all the corpses are cleaned out of the graveyard, he walks back to inspect his handiwork near the Great Door entrance. Everywhere he looks, corpses litter the landscape. Most of the bodies have landed on the ground; others dangle from tree limbs; and some actually stand up, leaning against objects, looking ominous and mysterious.

"Good. The chamber should be safe now," Flagrot says. He proceeds to walk back to the city of Pink Bosom.

*   *   *

Standing on his head, Pigfeeler tries to make the best of his imprisonment. The rats take no notice as they scamper to the next jail cell through the small gap under the door. The door outside the cell opens, and Pigfeeler can hear a clanking noise of heavy armor approaching. His jail door slowly opens, and the Pink Knight fills the doorway with his full, dominant presence.

"Do you know who I am?" the Pink Knight demands.

"The fully armored court jester?" Pigfeeler remarks.

"Why did you burn down the village?"

"I was filled with so much flammable cheer, there was no way I could hold a fire without hurting my being."

The knight quickly draws his sword, approaches, and cuts Pigfeeler's ear off. Pigfeeler falls onto his stomach and quickly grabs his bloodied head. "That is for the desecration of the village square. Now tell me why you burned those specific buildings?"

Pigfeeler holds his head tightly with both hands to stop the outpouring of blood. "I ... I can lead you to great power and riches."

The knight removes his helmet to reveal a strong war-driven face with a hardened mouth. He grabs Pigfeeler by his shirt and lifts him into the air. "Look into my eyes! Look!" the knight barks. "Repeat what you said while looking into my eyes."

Pigfeeler struggles to focus, but he eventually sees the cold blue eyes. "I can lead you to great power and riches."

"You actually believe it. Tell me more. Keep looking into my eyes!" the Pink Knight says as he shakes the little man.

"It's called the Great Door. I can show you where it is."

"No! Tell me where to find it!"

"I need to see the area to find it. The door is well hidden."

The Pink Knight throws Pigfeeler to the ground. Pigfeeler's back receives numerous scratches from the small, jagged floor stones.

"If I show you the door, will you drop any penalties against me?" Pigfeeler begs.

A sword blade wavers in front of Pigfeeler's throat. "What

will I need to conquer this Great Door?" the Pink Knight says in a loud whisper.

"An army."

The knight stares intently into Pigfeeler's eyes.

"The Great Door is so powerful that you will need an army to break through," says the shivering Pigfeeler. "And when you enter the Great Door, I want a piece of the treasure."

"What is the treasure?"

"I don't know, but it is so powerful and plentiful that even a small piece would satisfy my every dream."

The Pink Knight stares through Pigfeeler. The conquest of power fills the knight's mind. *Owning what is behind this Great Door could give me a huge advantage over his Snob competition for King Supreme Leader of the entire kingdom of the Sentient Noble Order of Bravery. I could bribe my way to the top.*

The Pink Knight grabs his helmet, sheathes his sword, and walks out of the jail cell. When he arrives outside, he says, "Messenger, run from town to town to gather my troops and purchase as many explosives as my army can carry." The Pink Knight looks down the center of the street to see the remnants of a long dong drawn in the dirt.

The Pink Knight's army of a thousand men approaches the body-filled area, which looks like a great plague has wiped out all sorts of creatures in the forest. Snob soldiers begin whispering their thoughts on the situation. "This place is cursed." "We will surely die!" "The smell—the awful smell."

The day fades into night, and everyone becomes extremely nervous with their surroundings.

"Keep marching men!" the Pink Knight orders.

Pigfeeler follows along, tied to the Pink Knight's horse. "This is the area, Pink Knight, sir. I am certain this is where the Great Door path begins. But the landscape has changed dramatically," Pigfeeler says with confusion in his voice.

The Pink Knight notices lots of movement in the bushes ahead. Something big is certainly building the paranoia of the army. "*Gather! Focus forward! Fire!*" the Pink Knight yells to his troops. All sorts of projectiles fly over the knight's head. Massive explosions fill the area where the innocent bush thrived. "*More! More!*" the Pink Knight demands. Fire and electricity annihilate the once-flourishing bush. The knight waves his army down, and the one-sided war stops. The Tazer Cannons screech a high, increasing pitch of reloading tazer balls, receiving an electrical charge. The area burns brightly as the knight guides his horse to inspect the damage. *This would have been a noble victory, had the target been a vicious beast and not a lost cow.* The Knight puts his left armor palm to his ashamed face.

Somewhere in the dusk of the setting sun, a soldier yells from the back of the army, "Over there! Something is moving!"

In the limbs of a tree is a corpse, dangling in the wind. Acting of its own accord, the army quickly destroys the unknown threat with ranged artillery.

"There!" another soldier yells. Then more soldiers see more threats. The soldiers become panicky as they tear open the entire forest around them. As explosions light the area, shadows resembling a potential enemy haunt the paranoid troops as they mutilate the vicinity.

Debris flies in all directions. A soldier with a fireball mini-launcher—a portable shoulder weapon with extreme incendiary potential—notices an object fly from the blazing surroundings into a military wagon within the army ranks. He turns his mini-launcher inward and screams for fire support. "I need help! Fire on my target!"

The wagon receives a rainfall of destructible munitions and quickly explodes with thunderous molten spray. The fire spreads to other wagons swiftly. As the Pink Knight notices the problem, all the wagons fill with explosive munitions and vaporize the entire army, leaving a gigantic crater that marks the end of the Snob assault on the environment.

Chapter 10
Capital F – Part 1

D uHero and Juulia's journey becomes unusually dangerous. They have to hide most of the time, as Boortards roam all along the Nymph territory boundary. As they hide in a cluster of trees, Juulia notices DuHero is focused intently on their surroundings.

"Where is your territory?" DuHero says.

"We are on it," Juulia whispers. "This forest is the boundary edge." Juulia points to a small clearing just outside of view. "The forest edge is the start of neutral territory over there. Well, at least informally between the races. Boortards have no laws or rules."

His sword is raised in guard-mode. Juulia never has had a man so close to her with the intent of protecting her being. She cannot resist the urge to kiss him under these stimulating, dangerous circumstances. As she turns quickly to face him, the blade she was holding in her right hand slits DuHero's waist between his armor. DuHero keels over as Juulia kisses the air where DuHero's lips used to be. DuHero falls to his knees, trying to cover his wound. Juulia is shocked at the blood.

They both think to themselves, *Did a Boortard attack?*

DuHero pulls his body out of his upper armor and quickly places his hands over the wound. As she looks at her bloodied weapon, Juulia realizes she has severely injured the only man she cares about.

Before she can claim her guilt, a Boortard suddenly appears behind Juulia. DuHero raises his sword and painfully thrusts the blade over Juulia's right shoulder and into the face of the intruder. She spins around to see the assassin fall dead at her feet. At a distance, two other Boortards witness the carnage. One of the trees near Juulia goes *thump-thump-thump.*

Juulia knows the sound. *Ranged arrows.* She takes cover tightly behind the tree as DuHero stands, trying to maintain a fighting posture. More arrows thump the wood as she notices a Boortard trying to flank their position. Juulia vanishes, to DuHero's amazement. He breathes heavily, trying to sustain the pain. Something fiery explodes behind the tree, and sparks litter the air. Then there is complete silence.

A minute later, Juulia appears, and she lifts DuHero's left shoulder with her body.

"We need to go," Juulia says.

They try to move quickly, but DuHero's wound does not fix itself fast enough. Juulia senses assassins closing in on her position. Before she can react, three Boortard assassins appear behind her. DuHero quickly pulls Juulia out of danger, only to receive six well-placed blades to his stomach and chest. Juulia cloaks herself once again to become invisible so she can get away. From a distance, Juulia can see DuHero's slumping body keel onto the chest of one assassin. His dying hands are able to grip the ring-like objects out of the fist-sized balls from the assassin's chest. The resulting explosion kills two of the Boortards. The third assassin is hurt but manages to stand. Juulia watches as the assassin somehow yanks a glowing ring from DuHero's hand. Juulia has been watching DuHero for many sunrises, and she is absolutely sure he wore no jewelry. The Boortard puts on the ring and suddenly grows twice his size, and he begins to glow. The Boortard jumps around like an idiot and starts dancing over DuHero's body. More Boortards approach the dancing fool. They all start jumping like bucking donkeys and showing special interest in DuHero's body. Juulia cannot retrieve DuHero's equipment and instead, quickly leaves the area, looking for the closest graveyard.

In the distance, Juulia can see DuHero running to her. She uncloaks to become visible to DuHero. "Turn around! Turn around, you naked fool, and keep running!" Juulia screams while pointing where to run. "We need to leave this place," she pants. "Boortards want you. Don't ask me why."

A few Boortards see the unusual jogging couple but do not take chase. Through forest, fields, and hedges, they keep a steady pace. Both breathe hard and deserve a rest, but Juulia insists they push on. "We are not far from a Nymph scout station. My sisters will help us."

DuHero is quite exhausted but tries to speak. "How ... how will they react to a sweaty naked man running toward them?"

Juulia suddenly stops to think. DuHero gladly sits down and rests on the grass in the small open expanse of dedicated grassland. "Oh, this is so comfortable to my rear end," DuHero says as he spread his limbs outward to expose his entire body in a relaxed comfortable pose.

Scenarios of deception against her sisters fill Juulia's mind until she sees DuHero. New fantasies obtrusively emerge.

"Juulia, come sit with me. The grass is so comfortable." He closes his eyes. "I could sleep here a thousand sunsets with you at my side."

Fantastic urges swell through her body as she walks closer to the sweaty, glistening man she so desires. Slowly, she starts undressing, ready to give herself freely to the only man she has ever loved—and then a horrific noise fills the air. Gathered blades fill Juulia's hands as she searches the immediate proximity of the field where a beast might attack. Her head bends down in disappointment when she learns the raucous threat was an exhausted, snoring DuHero.

Not understanding what is going on, DuHero finds Juulia

tying his hands together. She ties DuHero's legs with enough slack to allow him to walk normally but run terribly.

"You are my prisoner now. We need to make this look real so I can take you to Nympholymphus."

As DuHero is about to speak, multiple fists strike his face perfectly to cause the most swelling and bruising. His left ear suddenly goes missing. Juulia begins the trophy-chant and fits the new prize on her morbid belt.

"I am so sorry." Juulia leans down and kisses DuHero's bloodied lips. He winces a bit from the pain but a smile does shine through. The bleeding eventually stops. DuHero has the convincing appearance of a guest, ready for the Nymph prison system. Juulia helps DuHero stand, and he walks ahead. Juulia removes a small sword from the scabbard strapped to her back.

In the distance, a small, towering structure contains Nymphs in attack positions. Juulia forces DuHero to stop by tapping his shoulder with her blade. A strange wail of unknown words leaves Juulia's lips. A voice from the strong building replies. Juulia pushes DuHero forward and whispers, "Remember, you are my prisoner, so I need to torture you occasionally."

The Gooniness inside DuHero begins to thrive as ideas for his prisoner act give him the motivation to tolerate the punishment. Two Nymphs from the structure run up to DuHero, with daggers pointing at his chest. All the Nymphs exchange information through a language not too dissimilar to what DuHero understands. Juulia asks for a Robe of Protection, access to a PhishFone, and a flying creature capable of lifting three people and that can fly the long distance to the capital. The group moves slowly into the stone structure. DuHero is tied to a wooden stand near the stables.

Juulia leans in to DuHero's good ear. "Stay here and be good. You and I will be seeing the queen in the next few days."

DuHero looks into her eyes and gives a gaze of trust and understanding. She smiles slightly, turns, and walks toward a building which looks like a meeting room filled with chairs and a large table.

The stable has a small assortment of creatures that stare at DuHero. Some horses, a few large birds, and something that looks like a large beaver casually stand, waiting for attention.

A voice comes from the stable. "What is your name?" Before DuHero can look, a robe hits DuHero in the face and falls into his tied hands. The robe is hideously bright orange, with strange, large symbols loosely sewn into the eye-burning fabric. The Nymph guard pulls the robe over the previously naked man. She spanks him on the bottom and looks at his face sensually as she walks away.

"She likes you," the stable voice speaks again.

DuHero whispers, "Where are you? I cannot see you."

"I am the one with the big teeth and flat tail," the beaver says.

The only creature matching that description is the beaver. A beaver talks? I should not be surprised. After all, my best friend is a warrior pig.

"My animal form name is Rat. What is your name?" the beaver says.

"I do not have an animal name. Just my given name, DuHero."

"What is your crime, DuHero?" Rat says.

"Being a man, I suppose," DuHero says with hesitant contemplation. "Rat? Why Rat?"

"I was a Snob spy. I passed large amounts of information to my Snob superiors until I was discovered. My penalty? Being transformed into this beaver, given the asinine name of Rat. I am imprisoned for life, with hard slave labor; namely, delivering supplies to the outskirts of Nymph territory."

DuHero focuses on the beaver and notices the concealed wings on his back. "You can fly?" DuHero asks.

Rat unravels his wings slightly to demonstrate his capability. "Quite correct. They use me to haul heavy equipment to these outposts." Rat reads the symbols on DuHero's terrible orange fashion-wear and giggles. "They gave you the 'Do Not Kill' robe."

DuHero is puzzled as he lifts the robe to inspect the wording. "Is that what it says? Seems silly."

"Not at all. Nymphs have orders to kill or jail non-slave men within their borders. Well, except for young male children. Nymphs can control them easily."

"Do all Nymphs hate men so seriously?"

Rat laughs. "No. I believe most Nymphs despise the no-man laws set by the religious council. Before I was turned into a beaver, some Nymphs would secretly try to meet me. I wish they didn't chain me to the wall inside a prison cell. Some Nymphs who wanted me were so beautiful." Rat sighs and starts nervously nibbling on a stable beam support.

"Isn't it natural for men and women to be together?" DuHero asks with pure wonderment.

The beaver drearily turned his hairy head. "Of course. But the xenophobic religious council convinced the queen that fighting between men and women would stop."

Juulia approaches DuHero; a Nymph follows close behind. They walk past him and head to Rat. Saddles are mounted behind Rat's neck and strapped securely around the beaver's body. The Nymph yanks on the leash and leads the flying beaver outside the stable. Rat lowers his body, and DuHero is forced to sit on the front saddle, while Juulia mounts the rear saddle. When everyone is secured, Juulia takes a blade from her chest strap and mounts the lethal weapon in front of her saddle for easy access.

"Thank you, sister. I will take both these criminals to the queen."

DuHero tugs on Rat's neck-hair to get his attention. DuHero leans forward and whispers to Rat, "Criminal?" Rat turns his head and sees DuHero's confused face. He smiles, showing his big yellow teeth, and shrugs his silky-hair shoulders. Rat whispers back, "I did *something* bad … again. Welcome to Nymph territory and their bizarre legal system."

The Nymphs salute each other with a fisted arm pointed out diagonally and facing upward. With a pull of the reins, the beaver unravels and flaps his giant wings, and the group lifts wobbly into the air.

DuHero is visibly upset. He holds on anxiously to the saddle strap and tightens his legs.

"Hey! Not so hard. DuHero, you are crushing my ribs!" Rat bellows.

"Then fly better. Can't you be stable?" Juulia says.

"I am a beaver with wings. The witch who gave me this curse didn't understand the simple concept that *beavers do not fly*!" Rat scowls. His anger makes the ride more erratic. The group rises diagonally higher as the beaver tries to steer toward the Nymph capital. DuHero makes the mistake of looking down at the land beneath them. A suddenly frightened DuHero quickly wraps his arms around Rat's neck and squeezes tightly.

"Ackuckah … Stop chokagguhd …" the choking beaver tries to relay.

"Stop it, DuHero!" Juulia tries to pull DuHero off Rat; they spiral toward the ground. No one survives.

DuHero is still shaking with fear when they all appear at a graveyard.

"DuHero, you fool, you—" Juulia is interrupted by a surprising hug from DuHero. Tears stream down his face. She hugs back. Rat sees the opportunity to fly away while the humans are distracted. Rat finds the romantic drama more interesting than his freedom.

"Too high. We were too high," DuHero sobs. Juulia never expected to see such a callous strong man tremble in her arms. She feels comfort in caring for the emotional Goon.

Rat sees through their secret. "Well, now. You two are beyond hunter and prisoner. You two are in love."

Juulia feels the need to cut the beaver's throat, but then she realizes he is probably right. She continues to hold DuHero tightly. "Let's go, DuHero. We need to find our bodies and collect our equipment."

"Before we go …" The beaver slowly steps away from the hugging couple. "Promise me when we arrive near the capital, we will land in an isolated place so I can fly away."

Juulia is in no mood for deals, but she knows they need the beaver's assistance. "Why not fly away now?" Juulia asks.

The beaver sneers and studies the happy couple. "Receiving permission from a Nymph with your high rank would certainly help me escape long enough so I can fly far. But more important, I see you two starting a trend to fix a major problem in Nymph society. The Nymph authorities would probably be less concerned about my absence when compared to the problems you two will create."

DuHero does not listen, and Juulia is not sure of Rat's true intentions. Yet to her, the deal seems honest. "Agreed," Juulia reluctantly says.

The three recover their equipment and clothing from the sky-smashed bodies of their former selves. DuHero's clothing is heavily blood-covered, as are the saddles.

"Before we can travel, we need to remove the blood," Juulia says.

Rat scouts from the air and leads the humans to a small lake deep in a forest. When they arrive at the lake, Rat makes an unusual proposal. "Let me slobber on the robe and saddles. As a side effect, my internal fluids can be used as a cleanser."

Juulia looks away as the beaver snorts and spews fluids onto the bloodied equipment. Once Rat is finished, DuHero submerges the saliva-covered objects into the lake. The blood elegantly washes away.

Darkness approaches quickly. Juulia makes a fire from the wood DuHero collects and that Rat chews down to manageable pieces. DuHero and Juulia sit together, leaning against the beaver as he sleeps.

"I am sorry for killing us," DuHero says apologetically. "I had a feeling I experienced something similar in the past. But my memory robs me of actually knowing what happened."

Juulia gently takes hold of DuHero's hand.

"Juulia, why did you go with Flagrot to find that room?"

One of Juulia's duties as a Nymph agent to the Nymph queen is to never reveal the objective of the mission, but she feels DuHero should know. "Nymphs are voluntarily seeking permanent nirvana."

DuHero is shocked that Juulia has told him a secret, yet he tells her, "I do not completely understand."

"Nymphs are giving up their existence voluntarily. We call it self-extinction, or the act of existicide. The numbers of Nymphs existiciding have become significant."

"What is the difference between dying and existiciding?" DuHero says as his face strains. DuHero knows he needs to use his brain, but his desire to neutralize all thought is set too high. He pretends to listen.

Juulia sighs. This conversation hurts her insides. "Death is nothing more than a mistake we make in life. We can re-exist from our mistake and try again. Self-extinction is the choice made by an individual who does not want to re-exist. The most popular method of existicide is self-trophyism."

Finally, something DuHero understands. "The trophy-chant you used on my ear?" DuHero says.

"Yes. We can use a crystal that magnifies our power hundreds of times and point the trophy-chant on ourselves. Since the chanter becomes a trophy of her own making, she cannot break the chant, as trophies become suspended and lifeless."

DuHero's mind begins to race. The depth of this secret is profoundly intimate to Juulia. "There is no way to free them?" DuHero asks.

"Not really. I heard rumors that someone could, but our society respects the choices of our sisters, and we let them stay extinct."

"Is it a certain group of Nymphs who decide to choose self-extinction?"

Juulia stands to throw more wood on the fire. "No. The practice exists all throughout our society."

"What about children? Can't your society make more children to recover the losses?"

Juulia slams a log into the fire, sending sparks high into the air. "The foolish religious council created so many rules that make bearing and raising children nearly impossible. That is why we send many kids to Goon territory to grow up. Lesser of two evils, I suppose." Her voice becomes angrier, waking Rat. She continues. "We need permission from the queen just to pushim with a mate!"

DuHero assumes the word "pushim" means love. "Are we in pushim, Juulia?" DuHero innocently asks.

Rat and Juulia laugh. She falls to her knees and gives DuHero a big kiss. "No, you silly man. But I hope to someday."

Unknowing to DuHero, pushim, in the Nymph language, means "to have sexual intercourse with."

Rat chimes in, "Are you seriously going to ask your queen for permission?"

"I ... I have no choice. It is the law," Juulia says.

Chapter 11
Capital F – Part 2

The next day, the group spends most of their time flying toward the capital. Rat lands on the outskirts of the large city, and Juulia respects their deal. As Rat flies away, Juulia ties DuHero's hands together with a rope. They walk toward the city border.

Numerous beautiful buildings of varying colors garnish the capital. Every building has an original illustration of patterns, war scenes, or nature drawn upon the visible surface. Woman after woman stares attentively at Juulia's prisoner. DuHero expects unwarranted hatred from the females but instead, he witnesses curiosity, excitement, and perhaps lust. His masculine charm and smile cause some women to blush. His missing ear does not deter women from glancing, smiling, and even following the group. Juulia waves her hand to the oglers to keep their distance.

The two reach the magnificent towering stone palace, home to the queen, the religious council, and a number of important political representatives. A grand set of steps leads to the first large hall, which is lined with oversized statues on strong carved pedestals. DuHero looks at the spectacular creations as they enter a soaring, elongated hallway. DuHero is shocked at the staggering length and height of the corridor. The walls are filled with artistic creations of all styles. Juulia pushes DuHero forward to make him keep moving.

"Juulia, your culture is beyond fascinating," DuHero says.

"Be quiet!" she whispers.

They finally arrive outside of the great courtroom where the queen moderates major conflicts that are brought before her. Nymphs wait for their chance to see the queen, so Juulia makes DuHero sit on the ground while she hovers beside him.

A few hours pass, and then Juulia is allowed to see the queen. As they enter, many women who line the sides of the room focus their eyes on the rare masculine surprise. A man is in the sacred courtroom!

"Why did you bring this foul man into my court?" demands Queen Danashia.

The queen's throne sits gracefully on a six-step purple stone platform. The throne wall holds a fantastically complex pattern of shapes, symbols, and figures, molded in gold, dressed with diamonds, and stuffed with unknown objects found during Crazyrage season.

"Flagrot asked me to bring DuHero back to the capital and to protect me during my journey," Juulia says loudly, so the entire court can hear.

"That swine Flagrot," the queen says, while thinking to herself, *What is that old fool Flagrot up to?* "Flagrot was a fool to make such a request," the queen says.

Juulia is offended. "DuHero saved my life against Boortards."

"And you survived?"

"Yes. Their numbers were too great and for some strange reason, they celebrated DuHero's death. I believe they recovered something extremely valuable from his corpse."

"Something valuable from a dead man? Is it not the man's being dead that is the true value?" the queen jests. A few in the court hesitantly laugh at her attempt at morbid humor. She looks around to see a quiet courtroom. "Fine. Tell us what they found."

"A Boortard found a ring where none existed. When the Boortard placed the mysterious item on his finger, the Boortard grew in size, and he glowed."

"Why are we talking about this man and Boortards? I sent you on a critical mission. What did Flagrot give you to solve our crisis?"

Juulia bows her head slightly as a sign of respect. "We found the devices he was seeking. He is studying them now to find a solution."

"You mean the existicide problem?" DuHero blurts out.

The queen stands in anger. "How does this waste of skin know about our mission?" the queen says.

Juulia turns to DuHero and gives him a bitter look. She faces the queen. "I trust DuHero, so I told him about our blight."

The court murmurs.

"Another charge added to his sentence," the queen announces.

"Huh?" DuHero says with a nasal grunt. "What charge?"

Juulia becomes hostile. "My queen, he has done nothing wrong."

"His existence in our kingdom is forbidden by law," a religious council member speaks out. A group of seven well-dressed religious representatives fill the chairs at a hand-carved table at the side of the room near the queen.

"He is our guest. He wears the Robe of Protection, and I bound his arms to show that he can't harm us," Juulia says, while portraying her frustration by holding back her anger. She bows her head with respect. "My queen, I formerly request permission to pushim this man."

"No," the queen says.

"Can he touch my lower flesh fence?" Juulia says in a forceful tone.

"No," the queen says.

"My susu?"

"No."

"My eye bilong susu?"

"No."

"What about lips. Can we kiss?"

The religious council stands and scrunches together for an ad-hoc discussion. A few minutes later, the council members return to their seats.

"No," says a council member.

DuHero rolls his eyes, and Juulia clenches her fists.

The queen adds, "There is no point to being with this man. He will be locked in our jail for a very long time."

DuHero's head sulks at the horrific news. Before the queen dismisses the couple, DuHero slowly walks past the shocked Juulia and toward the queen. He speaks loud and clear: "I know how to solve your existicide problem."

The courtroom erupts with discussion. The queen raises her hand, and the room silences. "Speak, meathead."

DuHero does not flinch at the insult. "Your people, Nymphs, need men in their lives."

"Outrageous!" a council member yells spontaneously.

DuHero continues. "Nymphs need men to complement their strengths and cover their weaknesses."

The same council member yelps, "Nymphs work together to make a future for our kingdom. We need no men for such an accomplishment."

"Can two Nymphs make children?" DuHero asks with arrogant clarity.

"Irrelevant! Heretic!" comes from the council table.

"Bearing and raising children brings infinite joy to a couple. Children give responsibility, purpose, and belonging. But most important, love," DuHero says.

The court is abuzz with conversation. DuHero continues. "If Nymphs remove these sexual discrimination laws, along with laws that invade the bedroom, existicide rates should drop significantly, and more children will be born."

The courtroom is loud with discussion. Everyone has something to say, and debates become fierce.

A prominent-looking figure on the council stands to speak. Her large size and worn face of experience extol her dominance. "Long-term coupling has a 50 percent failure rate. This causes arguments and pain between people!" the tall woman says.

DuHero is ready. "Zero coupling has a 100 percent failure rate. There may be no conflict, but what you have now is no passion, no love, no children, and no life!"

Everywhere the discussions become heated. Even the women waiting for an audience with the queen hear the news and begin debating among themselves. The queen has never seen so much conflict in her court.

Grabbing the back of his robe, DuHero pulls the ugly clothing over his head and lets the orange cover drop to the ground. The room falls quiet with gasps as naked DuHero shows his defiance by raising his arms diagonally, along with his diagonal protrusion.

Many women gasp. This is the first time for many to see a man in his pure splendor.

DuHero speaks briskly. "I salute those who go against these terrible laws. To make my point clear, I would pushim you." He points to the Nymph guards. "And you." He points to the queen's servants. "And definitely you." He points to the queen. He pauses to look around and points to the religious council. "And even you, because you ladies need pushim the most."

Many in the court laugh but not the queen or the religious council. One member of the council blushes heavily.

"Kill him!" the dominant council member says with feverish resolve. "He removed the robe and disgraced the court. Kill him!"

Juulia pulls out her daggers and watches the council. A few court guards unsheathe their weapons. "Guards, kill that man!" "Kill!" "No mercy!" council members say, over-speaking each other. The guards do nothing except look to the queen for guidance.

The dominant council member instigating for DuHero's death suddenly finds herself with a dagger to her throat. The queen holds the weapon carefully in place.

"The queen decides who dies! Sit down and calm yourselves," the queen says as she delicately withdraws the blade.

Draped over one arm of the queen's throne, the queen's royal robe has been set aside quickly so she can move rapidly against the unruly council. The queen wears an outfit similar to Juulia's, with weapons strapped around her body and boots. The queen has no trophies on her belt. The queen sheathes her weapons and slowly walks to Juulia. "Juulia Estratra, you are one of my best warriors. Why do you defend this defiant man?"

Juulia does not let down her guard. "We fought as a team. We even fought each other. He has shared his feelings, his fears, and I trust him with my existence." She speaks firmly. "DuHero is correct. My personal frustrations all relate to the bad laws created by the council."

The queen speaks prudently. "Nothing has changed except your future in this court. Guards, take that rebellious man to jail."

DuHero quickly speaks to Juulia. "Juulia, I am severely afraid of jail cells. Please come with me; I need your support."

A guard retrieves the orange robe and places the attire over DuHero's head.

As DuHero and Juulia are escorted out of the presence of the queen, the queen pulls out a dagger and throws the weapon just over the heads of the religious council. The dagger wobbles in the pierced wood, just behind the now-shaking members.

The jail area is circular so that prisoners can see each other fade away to mental oblivion. DuHero is the only prisoner among the twenty cages. Anxiety builds as the metal-grid jail door shuts behind him. Juulia reaches in and grabs his right hand. Both hands meet with a careful embrace.

"Juulia, I may never come back. Jail cells turn me mad, and the person you know as DuHero may vanish."

They move closer together but are stopped by the cold bars. She lets go of him, gently grabs his head, and pulls him in for the kiss she so desired. She tries to put her hands around DuHero's large frame. The bars do not stop DuHero from embracing Juulia. The steel barrier between them reflects the emotional obstacles they will face in the future. "I will stay as long as I can. But I will need to leave to find a way to release you."

"No. No. No," DuHero whines. "I cannot be alone. I died in a jail before. I will turn into a lunatic and nobody will ever release me because of my condition."

The young female guard sitting in the center of the room cannot hold back her tears. Juulia turns to her. "My sister, could you come here?" Juulia asks politely.

The guard wipes away her tears and picks up her short spear. As the young female guard walks to her, Juulia says, "What is your name, sister?"

"Tammyana Preesland," says the cautious guard.

"I am Juulia Estratra, high warrior general to the queen."

"I know who you are."

"Tammyana, would you help me take care of DuHero? This man has a profound fear of jail cells."

Tammyana immediately answers, "Men are bad and not to be trusted."

"This man is special. He is harmless to you. He just needs someone to hold so he can feel secure."

"If this is a trap, I warn you, I do not have the key to his cell," Tammyana says.

"I promise you, this is not a trap. If you take care of DuHero, I will be in debt to you."

As Tammyana looks at DuHero, she can see the grave despair in his lost eyes.

"DuHero, let Tammyana take your hand. She will hold it while I am gone."

Both hesitate. "I ... I never touched a man," Tammyana says as she reaches out and carefully clasps DuHero's large hand, which is still holding Juulia. Juulia steps back slightly.

DuHero slowly complies, as does Tammyana.

"Don't be scared. Feel free to talk," Juulia says.

"Feel free." DuHero chuckles at the dark humor.

"I will be back. Thank you, Tammyana."

Day after day, DuHero's hand always reaches out of his cell, looking for comfort. When Juulia cannot satisfy DuHero's need for physical contact, female guards sit with DuHero, talking to him and holding his hand. DuHero tells each guard of his unusual short life, while female guards tell DuHero about their problems. He listens, gives empathy, and always thanks them for their support.

Today will not be a normal day. Noises can be heard from the hallway to the circular jail. The female guard releases her grasp of DuHero's hand and runs to grab her sword and steel prison keys. The hallway door bursts open. Two guards restrain a large, muscular woman. She is locked in a cell opposite of DuHero's cell, and profanities fill the room. The young female guard stands in the center of the room, staring at the new prisoner. When the escort party leaves the prison room, she drops her sword and shield and quickly grabs DuHero's hand.

"I am sorry, DuHero," the young guard says.

"I understand, Kimantha. You have duties," DuHero says.

"Hey! That's a man!" the burly prisoner roars.

DuHero stands while holding the guard's hand. "Hello. My name is DuHero. What is your name?"

The new prisoner notices the orange uniform and laughs. "I am Beglinda Zarch, I am a beast hunter." Although DuHero has the body of a strong man, his face shows the deep sadness of a troubled child. Beglinda's tone softens. "Why are you here?"

"I am here because I am a man."

Beglinda proudly announces, "I am here for openly expressing my feelings."

"Expressing feelings? That is not illegal," Kimantha says.

"I had the feeling that the tax collector needed a slap to her face," Beglinda says joyously.

They all talk late into the night. Beglinda asks if she can help with the hand-holding duties. Kimantha is willing to move Beglinda to a cell beside DuHero. Beglinda promises to cooperate, with DuHero's approval. Kimantha slips out and retrieves the cell door keys from a room down the hall. The transfer is successful, and the guard returns the key before anyone notices.

DuHero sleeps, holding Beglinda's hands.

Both are happy to see him rest—until the snoring starts.

Chapter 12
Goon Vomit

After an unceremonious vomit on the meeting table, Refailable slumps down in his recliner throne. "You Flaggots, why am I here? I want to kill you all and … uugh." His sudden upheaval turns the contents of his shirt into the same foul décor as the recently vomit-graced table.

"Here, dear fat leader," one member says as he slaps a glazed ham in Refailable's lap. "Ham is good for over-drink head pain."

Refailable wearily grabs the ham, takes a bite, and throws the chunk mass at the nose of the notes taker. He shrugs off the pain, like ham has hit his head in the past.

"Refailable, just sit there and hold your dong. Let us start the meeting. We have lots of news," says the Minister of Trade and Greed.

"*Gooniness!* I want to hear Gooniness!" demands the barely sober leader of the entire Goon kingdom. The Minister of Miscellaneous Flaggotry sighs and then speaks. "Goon activities include the usual legal demands for nudity to be mandatory while dancing, body-hair burning contests, speed contests for consuming acid before death, and the worst of all, bad poetry readings to spiked dead-bunny audiences."

"Pfft. Not bad," Refailable mumbles as he wipes last night's feast from his chin. "Oh, oh, oh, who won the dong-building tournament? How high was it?"

"The monument was quite ingenious. Micker Schlub placed four large balls as a foundation for his massive concrete dong."

"Typical. Artistic license combined with engineering. All right, proceed with your boring meeting," Refailable grumbles as he grabs a handful of puke from his shirt and flings the bile mass on the meeting table. The notes taker receives most of the stinky slop. The Minister of Wrecking Stuff leaves of the room.

"I will start with the mild news," says the Minister of Miscellaneous Flaggotry. "The bunny festival is dying. Bunnies are now seen scattered all over Forever, except Goonland."

Nobody realizes a bunny is hiding behind a barrel in the meeting room. The white fuzzy creature gathers all the details of Goony secret plans.

"We recommend the bunny festival be officially declared successful and finished," the minister concludes.

Refailable doesn't move or care. The Minister of Miscellaneous Flaggotry moves on to the next matter for discussion. "Flagrot is organizing the biggest festival in the history of Forever. He requests that every Goon contribute to the festival by gathering materials so our crafters can shape them into various props, weapons, mini-shelters for merchants, and many other items. He is quite serious about making this very memorable, and he has picked a festival site far away from Goonland, so we can promptly destroy the area with our party shenanigans. But, we are not sure how receptive the other races will be to joining the festival."

The Minister of Being Sneaky interjects, "Our spy reports, although very interesting, lead me to believe the Nymphs and Snobs may not attend."

The minister who left the meeting earlier enters the room with two buckets of water. Everyone hurriedly saves their parchments as the first bucket splashes over the table, cleaning the mess. The notes taker is the only one soaked with water and diluted vomit.

A second splash is aggressively hurled at Refailable. As expected, the wobbly leader, who is now wet and clean, chases the Minister of Wrecking Stuff with a worn blade that he quickly fumbles and drops. The ham is used as a projectile, but ham does not travel well, like an iron catapult ball. Refailable retreats to his throne as the minister finds his own seat.

The Minister of Being Sneaky continues. "As usual, we do not have much useful information on the Porcs. Our burning village espionage turned into comedy as the Pink Knight somehow became involved in a quest to completely destroy his army and himself by blowing up their munitions wagons."

The group laughs hard at the unusual news. The minister continues. "The last time we saw the Pink Knight, he was walking back to Snob territory in peasant clothing."

Refailable smoothly asks, "Did the burning of the syndicate-owned buildings and his losing his army permanently ruin his glorious reputation?"

"Indirectly. But we believe the Pink Knight will use scare-mongering to incite fear in his people and cover his army losses. With panic on the mind of Snob citizens, they may not attend the festival."

"Why do we care about this syndicate?" the Minister of Inventing Bits of Junk asks.

"The syndicate is the true power behind the Snob hierarchy," the Minister of Being Sneaky says. "The Pink Knight, we believe, is a pawn ... knight ... pawn ... whatever. We think he is being groomed by the syndicate to become a future king."

"If the Pink Knight becomes king, then Goons are doomed to long-term boredom and self-destruction," the Minister of Wrecking Stuff adds.

The Minister of Inventing Bits of Junk still does not understand but makes a guess. "So ... the Pink Knight, being well-experienced with Goon behavior, will ..." He tries hard to think like a political manipulator. "He will never go to war with us, and Goons, being Goons, will war with themselves."

"Correct. Goons always need an enemy and if one cannot be found, then Goons will fight amongst themselves," the Minister of Being Sneaky says.

"Now that the bunny-killing festival is over, what is preventing Goons from going to civil war right now?"

Many ministers look to the fat Refailable, who is picking his nose determinedly.

"Because I am great Goon!" Refailable says with flatulent exuberance.

"Our leader is a cult personality that Goons respect and love. His … symbolism … gives Goons a common man to love and hate," the Minister of Being Sneaky says.

"But I hate always doing stuff for Goons. Bunch of whiny brats needs so much attention," Refailable adds with surprising clarity. "A good long war will keep the Goons off my back, or I will rage-quit and let Goonland fall into self-destruction." He notices a nasal treat on his finger and promptly eats the unidentified surprise. "Whatever, not my problem. Ministers do all work." Refailable re-states his contempt for the meeting.

The Ministers look at each other with slight puzzlement and weariness. "The Nymphs are in a revolt, thanks to a Goon," the Minister of Being Sneaky says.

The members turn their heads to the speaking minister. Refailable actually becomes interested. "A Goon? Wonderful! How big is the revolt?" Refailable says.

"Very big by now. Last reports tell me Nymphs started burning down religious buildings and drawing strange 'F' graffiti all over their kingdom."

Refailable smiles for the first time today. "Who is this Goon, so I can give him a big man-hug and squeeze his butt cheeks?"

The minister pauses, knowing their leader will not like the answer. "DuHero caused the revolution," the Minister of Being Sneaky says, with hesitation.

Refailable slams both fists on the table and donkey-kicks his recliner throne.

While Refailable destroys the contents of the room, the spying bunny darts behind the stacks of junk and resources to avoid being discovered. The ministers speak quietly among themselves as tools and small boxes fly around the room. When Refailable becomes exhausted, the Minister of Miscellaneous Flaggotry speaks. "Since Nymphs are busy with a revolution, their presence at the festival will probably not exist."

Refailable picks up a scattered chair and walks to the table. "Give Flagrot what he needs for the festival. If no one else comes, then it will be a huge Goon party, and we can destroy the area. May Goonocracy thrrrruhhh ..." Refailable throws up the last contents of his stomach and collapses on top of the medium-sized notes taker. The small man cannot move and can barely breathe, as he is pinned to the table by a stinking, drooling Goon with too much power. During his agony, the ministers leave the room. After many moments of being alone with a sleeping rage-machine crushing his back, the notes taker sees a small bunny dart out of the room. The bunny scampers away to relay the Goon news to his superiors.

Chapter 13
Capital F – Part 3

More and more prisoners start filling the cells. This high level of imprisonment is quite unusual for Nymphs. As another young prisoner is led into the prison room, she notices DuHero and becomes excited.

"It's him! It's the symbol! Freedom for Fornication!" she shrieks and raises her tied arms. "Please, sisters. Put me in with him." She turns to the guard and makes a face of innocence. The guard promptly ignores her request but allows the overjoyed prisoner to have a cell beside DuHero. Beglinda does not mind the roommate, but she is reluctant to give up DuHero's hand.

"Beglinda, let the young one join us," DuHero says.

Squeezing in front of Beglinda, the new woman tells everyone her name: Selation Lantish.

The huddled group exchanges information and pleasantries. What Selation says next shakes DuHero's soul to the core. "DuHero, your behavior started a civil war among Nymphs. You are the direct cause of the revolution."

"Revolution? I have been trapped here for weeks," DuHero says in puzzlement. "The only people I talked to who have access to the outside are Juulia and the guards who watch this room."

Selation is so excited to be talking to DuHero that she almost forgets to breathe.

"Please relax," DuHero says as he gives a hand to her. "Please tell me more."

Selation finally gains her composure. "DuHero, your exhibition in the queen's court has given hope to a better life for many Nymphs, if the sexual discrimination and sexual permission laws are removed. Many Nymphs are actively protesting, rebelling, and spreading the word. The queen has been arresting individual protesters, like me, but there will be more going against her."

The prisoners who hear the news are happy and congratulate him.

Selation continues. "You are also a symbol for the revolution. Your symbol is showing up all over the capital and outer villages in the vicinity."

"How am I a symbol?"

On the sandy ground, Selation draws a vertical line and a dot on top. At the top of the line, she draws a diagonal line to the upper right. She does the same again in the middle of the vertical line.

"I am an excited capital letter F?"

"Heh, you are cute. See, the dot is your head; the vertical line is your body and legs. The upper diagonal line is the Nymph salute and the—"

Laughing roars throughout the jail cell. Selation speaks louder.

"That letter 'F' means that we look at you from the side. It also means Freedom for Fornication, Family First, and other wonderfully obscene 'F' words."

DuHero is stunned and shocked, but others in the room laugh, chat, holler, and cheer.

More and more prisoners fill the cells. DuHero is the only prisoner without a roommate. Many of the prisoners are classified as enemies of the kingdom and are told they are going to receive the penalty of extinction. Many don't care. Their lives were empty before the revolution and hopelessness set in; the revolution gave them a purpose. Now, at the very least, they will receive martyrdom status if the queen begins extincting her people.

DuHero continues to learn from each new prisoner. The revolutionary stories escalate in violence, deception, and civil war. Many religious symbols related to the entendre eminence of the religious council have been defaced, scarred, melted, shattered, and—the most interesting—reformed into a dong.

Worship and administrative buildings are ransacked, burned, exploded, or frozen solid. One building holds hundreds of piglets that eat and deface everything in their path. Many Nymphs do not realize this is a Goon prank with bad timing. DuHero wonders if Juulia is part of this espionage. Capital guards clash with mobs of sexually frustrated Nymphs, and the guards lose many battles. Most of the graveyards are under rebel control, so fallen capital guards are captured and cannot return to duty. Many religious services are canceled or receive few parishioners. The queen is in constant session, with hundreds of Nymphs wanting to see her. The more patient, passive Nymphs lobby the queen and political representatives to change the laws.

Every new prisoner has a new story. Each day, another extravagant incident builds the morale of the prisoners. Many merchants refuse to sell their goods to the palace or religious institutions. There is lots of food and supplies for the rebels, children, and anyone not affiliated with fighting against the rebellion. Another prisoner is brought into the prison room. The prison guard at the table says she will put her in a cell. The escort guards are glad to leave the prisoner. They quickly run out of the prison room. The prison guard turns her nose as she grabs the prisoner's arm and guides her close to DuHero. As the cell door next to DuHero is opened by the guard, a small package falls down between the new prisoner's legs. She kicks the package swiftly into DuHero's cell. Everyone in the vicinity holds their noses as a horrific fish smell emanates from the new prisoner.

"Echh. You stink beyond comprehension. You need to be

cleaned," the prison guard says. She goes to a wooden supply cabinet and throws a bar of soap at the fish-stinking woman. As she undresses and the guard goes to gather water, DuHero carefully takes the package and hides it under his robe. Beglinda is the only one who notices the package, and she remains silent.

Fish stink begins to disappear from the air, although the package has remnants of something fish-like. DuHero continues his routine of asking new prisoners their names and their crime.

"My name is Heathera, the fisher lady, and my charge is slapping the face of a religious council member with a large mackerel." All the Nymphs in the room laugh. Even the jail cell guard smiles as she returns with the bucket of water and places it beside Heathera's cell. "The foolish capital guards chased me without realizing I was a distraction. The religious council member was kidnapped as I was caught."

The guard looks at Heathera. "Don't you know I need to report a serious crime like that?"

"Go ahead," the defiant Heathera jests. She gyrates her naked body in a provocative, dirty dance. "I was ready to receive extinction long before the revolution. At least this way, I get to have fun."

The guard sighs. "You could receive a long prison term."

"Unlikely. A large group of us existicider members will fill your jails to a point where the queen has no choice but to release us or extinct us."

Everyone is silent. Heathera continues. "By the way, we kidnapped eight out of ten high-council religious members."

The guard quickly leaves the room to report the news to her superiors. Heathera asks Beglinda if she can speak with DuHero alone. When Beglinda complies, Heathera holds DuHero's hand and whispers, "DuHero, I have a message from Juulia. She is sorry she couldn't see you. She is being hunted as a traitor to the kingdom."

Worry fills the big man's face. Heathera continues. "She is

fine. She sent me here with the package. Keep it hidden under your robe. Contact her using the PhishFone."

DuHero slowly opens the package. He sees a small fish enclosed in a case filled with thick fluid. He picks up the boxed fish. "I never used this thing before," DuHero whispers back.

"Say 'Hello, PhishFone. I am DuHero. Can I talk to Juulia please?'"

DuHero follows the exact instructions, and the fish speaks back in a somewhat high-pitched gurgling yet wispy voice. "Hello, DuHero. I am PhishFone Unglug, whisper breed. Establishing connection, please wait."

DuHero patiently waits.

"Connection complete. Enjoy your conversation," the fish says.

"Hello, DuHero. I missed you," Juulia whispers.

DuHero is shocked to hear the fish speak in Juulia's voice.

"Wow. Juulia, are you now a fish?"

Laughter emanates from the mouth of the fish. "No, I am normal. The PhishFone helps us communicate over vast distances."

"So the fish sounds like me at your end?"

"Yes."

"I am so glad we can talk. I was worried. Are you well?"

"I am safe, but you won't be. My rebel contacts inform me that you will receive extinction along with many prisoners. We need to break all of you out of prison."

DuHero goes through the package while they talk. He notices a small children's toy. "Oh, oh. I see you sent me a small bear."

"Yes, I know about your shenanigans. I forgive you."

As DuHero smiles, the fish smiles back. "How do I escape?"

Juulia does not hesitate. "Kill yourself."

DuHero pauses, unsure how to take the command. Then he realizes her plan. "For some reason, my chants do not work in this place," DuHero says, whining softly.

"Of course not. You are in a palace jail. The entire area is protected from unauthorized chanting."

"What do I do?"

"In the package you will find a bottle of pills, a pad of paper parchment, and a writing utensil. I already wrote a message on the papers. Take one pill and place it in the center of the paper. Fold it up so the pill does not fall out."

DuHero reads the message:

The queen is planning to extinct all of us in prison.
Swallow this pill when DuHero swallows his pill. We are escaping.

"Be ready to pass out all the pills, if you can, with the message," Juulia orders. "But not yet. Only when I contact you in the future."

"How does dying help us?"

"We will take over the palace graveyard jail. Keep the PhishFone close to you. Good-bye DuHero."

DuHero suddenly becomes sad. "Thank you, Juulia. Good-bye." He turns his head. "Thank you, Heathera. I will need both hands for a while." He lets go and proceeds to fold each paper note with a pill inside.

Explosions can be heard outside. Although there are no windows in the prison room, Nymphs with war experience can distinguish the sounds. As DuHero holds Heathera's hand again, the PhishFone speaks. "Hello, DuHero. I am PhishFone Unglug, whisper breed. Juulia wishes to establish a connection. Will you accept?"

"Yes," he whispers.

"Connection complete. Enjoy your conversation."

"Juulia? Juulia, are you there?"

"Yes, DuHero."

"Are you well? We heard many explosions."

"We are close to the palace graveyard jail. Pass out the notes."

"Understood." DuHero turns to Heathera. "Heathera, ask the guard for a bucket of water so you can wash your hair."

Heathera does as she's asked. The guard leaves the room.

DuHero stands. "Everyone, pass these around to each person and take one. We need to escape immediately, but wait for me to start." DuHero hastily passes the pilled messages to Heathera. The packages quickly go around the cell chamber. Everyone reads the message, waits, and watches DuHero.

The PhishFone speaks. "Now, DuHero. Get everyone to take the pill."

DuHero speaks to the prisoners. "I am taking the pill now and sitting at the back of my cell. Follow my instructions."

Everyone in the cell block voluntarily dies except one Nymph. "Guard! Guard! They are escaping!" the last living prisoner yells.

The prison guard calmly unlocks the prison room door and puts the water down near Heathera's cell.

"They are dead! They are escaping!" the last living prisoner says with angst.

"Why should I listen to you?" the guard grumbles.

"I am a spy for the queen. Look around at all the slumped bodies."

The guard scans the cells, reaches into the air above the central table, and starts pulling an invisible rope. The sounds of heavy, stomping boots fill the hallway outside. Five prison guards enter the room. They check the bodies.

"Send guards to the graveyard jail," a guard says.

Hand-to-hand battles between fallen palace guards and prisoners shove DuHero around the graveyard. Juulia attempts to hand out weapons to her fellow rebels when the queen and her ten personal guards enter the unlocked morbid jail block. The queen points to Juulia, and the guards begin running toward her. Four guards fall instantly as Juulia unleashes her throwing blades into their skulls. A few seconds later, three more fall to the ground from arrows in their necks. The fourth arrow misses the target but flies to the queen, who easily deflects the stray projectile with her forearmor. The robe covering the queen falls to the floor, along with the rest of her personal guards. Juulia and the queen eye each other intensely. A barrage of flying blades whooshes toward Juulia, who jumps and allows the deadly payload to hit Nymphs behind her. As Juulia lands, the queen tries to raise her customized six-shot crossbow, but her hand is met by a swing slice that opens the skin along her arm. DuHero watches the two exchange fantastic attacks and demonstrate superior dodging skills. Their flexibility and speed almost blurs except for the occasional pause of a wound or successful strike. The fighting between prisoners and guards ceases as everyone watches the blood-filled contest between high-status sisters. More palace guards pile into the area and watch the battle. Juulia successfully kicks the queen in the bottom, and she lands face-first on the ground.

DuHero sees a chance to be useful. He sits on the queen's bottom and plops his body down along her back, like a comfortable bench. He whispers a tickle-chant and the queen begins laughing hysterically.

The palace guards try to save the queen but the bloodied Juulia is ready to kill the fresh troops.

"I concede! I concede! Please stop!" the giggling queen asks with slight desperation.

The tickling stops. DuHero moves his naked body off the queen and stands. The queen follows, still grinning from her experience.

"Juulia, DuHero, walk with me at my side," the queen insists as she checks her wet wounds. She turns to the staring masses. "Assemble my court representatives. Everyone follow behind me." The queen recovers her royal robe and gives the gold-and-white patterned purple robe to DuHero. He graciously accepts and wears the outfit, noticing its heavy weight. The three walk together through the long halls. "You two have caused numerous problems in my kingdom." An explosion is heard outside. "Yes. That must be a pink pipe bomb. The rebels have been throwing those explosive devices at the palace," the queen says as she inspects her arm wound.

"Pink pipes? Why pink?" DuHero asks.

"A blend of masculine and feminine symbolism," the queen replies. Juulia tries to contain her laughter but cannot help smirking. "DuHero, your diagonal protrusion is an explosive," the queen says.

He pauses to think, but then his eyes bulge with shock. "I am sorry, Queen Danashia. I never expected this to happen," DuHero says calmly.

"I was somewhat certain. I hated the bad laws, too," the queen whispers strongly to her new compatriots.

"My queen," Juulia says, sounding confused, "why did you not fix the problems?"

The queen grasps DuHero's and Juulia's arms and pulls them in and whispers, "The religious council has numerous powers over me." They reach the courtroom where her servants, ministers, and war leaders are assembled. "Follow me to the open window," the queen says as she leads them toward a large bank of windows along one wall. DuHero observes the random fires, destroyed buildings, and large flying birds in the sky, dangling something unrecognizable. "See those birds with the packages? I am informed the packages contain the extinct bodies of the religious high council. Is this true, Juulia?"

"Yes. We wanted to show everyone how far the rebellion progressed."

"Did you capture the entire council?"

"No. We could not find two members."

"Juulia, if you take the council far away from the kingdom, I will throw out their absurd laws."

"Agreed," Juulia says, and a smile breaks through the tension in her face. Juulia pulls out a PhishFone from a tightly strapped bag on her side and contacts her rebel generals. The birds carrying the bodies fly off, and the random explosions stop.

"I will announce the changes now," the queen says. She walks to her throne and stands in front of it. "My subjects, my sisters. From this day on, the religious council is abolished. The laws created by the council for sexual discrimination and permission to copulate are now void. Their other laws will also be reviewed."

Shrieks of excitement and joy echo throughout the courtroom. The queen is privately ecstatic to be in control again. She slowly sits on her throne, watching the spontaneous celebrations. Her concentration is broken by thumping against her throne. She curiously walks around her seat of power to see Juulia and DuHero practicing their newfound freedom intimately. The queen smiles and walks back to her seat, thinking to herself, *I need pushim badly.*

Deep in the night, eight bird riders carry their packages over a vast distance to their ordered rendezvous. In the faint blue light of their glowsticks, eight religious leaders can be seen being dropped into the ocean and forgotten.

Chapter 14
Repairs

The walk back to Snob kingdom is notoriously painful to the ego of the Pink Knight. His troops look like a parade of tired peasants with damaged morale. Everything that was valuable, useful, or memorable has been completely destroyed by the large, fiery explosion. Previously, no matter how much they checked the ruins of their death, nothing could be salvaged except large clumped masses of fused metal.

When the soldiers reach the Snob border, the men go their separate ways to find their homes and loved ones. The Pink Knight does not care about their motives. He is heavily in thought, trying to contrive his next move to recover his pride from his dishonorable and expensive death. He starts a conversation with himself:

There is no way I can hide the accident. Many of the royal horses ran off after re-existence. The heavy weapons and equipment wagons belonging to my syndicate employer was vaporized, and my last suit of pink armor cannot be identified. He laughs. *So much lost. I need to find and access that Great Door. I need much more resources and better planning. Who can I blame for this mess? A new unknown Goon super-weapon?* He hurries his pace as ideas fly in his head. *I can't blame that idiot Pigfeeler.*

162

Who was that chanter he hated? Flushot? Flagsnot? Flagrot! A smile appears on his insidious war-weary face. *I do not know of this Flagrot, but I am sure someone at court will identify the Goon. Yes! I know what to do!*

After another day of walking, he arrives at his well-endowed home and finds suitable clothing for addressing the court. He quickly fixes his hair, eats some dried meat, and then hastily walks to the central castle. He moves slow enough not to sweat or display any indication of desperation, both shunned actions by Snobs. As he approaches the main castle gates, soldiers salute. A salute is returned as he storms in the doors. The polished marble structure gleams of wealth and cleanliness. The towering pillars guide the hallway path as his boots echo his clomping approach to the king's throne. A line of waiting Snobs patiently stands for their opportunity to speak to the king. The Pink Knight by-passes the line and marches directly into the addressing circle and loudly speaks his mind. The Pink Knight kneels and says with serious emphasis, "My king, forgive me for my hasty rudeness. I have most important news that requires your immediate attention. May we speak in private?"

The king has never liked the Pink Knight. He sees the knight as an immediate and direct threat to his throne. "No," the king coldly replies.

"Very well, Your Highness," the knight says as he stands. "The Goons are using an unknown super weapon."

The king waves off the previous discussion. The noble man within the talking circle steps out of the circle and stops. The king points to the Pink Knight to move into the center of the addressing circle, a man-length ring of red that, by law, allows a lower-status person to talk with the king. The Pink Knight complies.

"Tell me what you know," the king growls.

"Your Highness, I was investigating the devastating fires in the village of Dunice. Over half the buildings were burnt to the ground. I captured a Goon who was abandoned by his espionage party. The Goon told me to find a Goon named Flagrot because he was their espionage leader. I gathered my armies and headed into the neutral zone to find this powerful chanter. We arrived in an area full of dead bodies that were scattered over a large forest area. Our armies spotted Flagrot. Before we could kill or apprehend the chanter, my entire army of a thousand men was instantly destroyed."

Those who could hear the story demonstrated their shock with audible gasps and words of distress.

"Flagrot's weapon was so powerful, nothing could be salvaged. Our bodies didn't exist. Not even bones were left behind."

The king bellows to the audience, "Does anyone know of this Flagrot?"

An elderly man approaches the circle. "I, your boldness. He is a Goon with multiple skills in chants and inventions. He will be organizing the grand festival later this season."

"Sire," the Pink Knight says aggressively, "if you lend me the proper armies to capture Flagrot, we could learn of this super weapon."

"When is this festival, servant?" the king asks.

"No date has been set, Sire. We will receive ample warning because the festival will be much larger than previous celebrations."

The king begins to take serious interest. "Tell me why Snobs go to this festival."

The old servant pauses to carefully arrange his thoughts. "All the major races and cultures attend the festival to trade goods, share, learn, and celebrate their differences. There are contests, new inventions, games of skill, drink—"

"Enough!" the king says with authority. "Tell me the *real* reasons why important leaders and thinkers attend."

"Satisfying personal agendas is what truly attracts everyone. Snobs go to fight for glory and learn from our enemies. Nymphs seek mates for impregnation because men are disallowed in their kingdom. They also bring children so they can play together and see their fathers. Goons love to show off, fight, drink, eat, puke, and put on talentless shows. I believe they study the other races to see if they can incite chaos for their own amusement. I am not entirely sure why Porcs attend."

"Sire, the festival is a perfect opportunity for Flagrot to create massive devastation to all the races. We must be prepared," the Pink Knight insists.

The king spends a moment contemplating. "Knight, take a scout from the Royal Reconnaissance Guild. Show him the place where you lost your army. When he confirms your story, then we will prepare for war."

"As you wish, Sire. Thank you," the knight says.

"*Next!*" the king says violently.

*   *   *

Tabby is once again on a mission for Flagrot. The written instructions guide Tabby to a remote, undesirable corner of Forever, between Goon and Nymph territories. A mountain range in the distance slowly appears, growing larger as he walks toward the formidable barrier.

"You! Stop!" a raspy voice says.

Tabby complies. A Manbaby slightly larger than Tabby slowly peeks out from behind a wind-wrecked tree.

"My name is Tabby. I have peaceful intentions," Tabby says calmly.

The Manbaby slowly drags a large damaged stick as he fully appears in Tabby's sight. The Porc is not worried; he believes the Manbaby cannot skillfully yield weapons. Beating and crushing things to death are the Manbaby's only battle specialties. "Are you Tabby, DuHero's friend?" the Manbaby asks politely.

"Yes, I am," Tabby replies sincerely.

"Tabby!" the Manbaby yells. He drops the thick stick and moves to hug Tabby. Normally, Tabby's instinct is to kill fast-approaching creatures. But Flagrot gave strict instructions that his mission was diplomatic and confrontation was unacceptable. Tabby feels Flagrot gives him challenging tasks to enhance his character, along with accessing his personal strengths.

Strange. This crushing hug is giving me solace and a sense of belonging.

Tabby is lifted off the ground and carried a far distance toward the mountain range. In a melodic tone, the Manbaby sings over and over and over again:

DuHero's friend. DuHero's friend. I have DuHero's friend.
DuHero's friend. DuHero's friend. I have DuHero's friend.

As they enter an overgrown forest, Tabby sees a small light in the distance that struggles to penetrate the dark wood canopy. The DuHero song becomes louder. In the distance toward the light, a choir of Manbabies repeats the same lyrics, invented by his happy manly transportation.

Tabby is placed down near the forest edge. He slowly walks to the light and is amazed at what he sees. Hundreds of Manbabies face and stare at Tabby.

"Flagrot was correct. All the Manbabies must have moved here," Tabby whispers to himself. Tabby raises his right arm and waves. "Hello, everyone."

In unison, every Manbaby replies, "Hi, Tabby!"

Tabby smiles. "Do you have a leader? I would like to talk with him."

"Sure!" the Manbaby swarm replies in unison, while staring intently at Tabby.

A section of the crowd parts and a Manbaby walks towards Tabby. The leader looks like any other Manbaby. He has no unique clothing, marks, symbols, jewelry, or weapons. Nothing demonstrates his Manbaby authority.

"I am Squishslug. Welcome, DuHero's friend," Squishslug says articulately.

"Hello, Squishslug. I am called Tabby. Can we talk?"

"Follow," the Manbaby leader instructs. The crowds disperse in unison. They walk into a village made of stacked trees and mud. The shelters are large and badly constructed.

"Flagrot again was correct," Tabby mumbles. *Flagrot predicted a number of situations I might face. So far, with this knowledge, diplomatic relations should be easy to obtain.*

They enter an unsafe-looking shack. Tabby notices the home contents have nothing to reflect Squishslug's responsibilities. They sit on a ragged blanket that smells like a used Manbaby diaper.

"Squishslug, we need the Manbabies' help," Tabby says.

"*No!* We are not Manbabies anymore," the leader grumbles. "We each call ourselves 'Man.'"

My first sentence already jeopardized the talks. Good move, Tabby. Tabby remembers what Flagrot told him to do in case discussions went bad. "My apologies. Please forgive me for my mistake."

Squishslug smiles.

"I need your help. I am willing to teach you woodworking, stonecutting, and metalworking skills so you can build your own homes."

"We have homes," Squishslug responds quickly.

"When the cold, rainy, or Crazyrage season comes, your homes may not be strong or warm enough. Crazyrage will destroy your village. Your Men could make caves in the mountain, which will give you lots of protection and warmth."

"Can you teach us how to make fire safe in the home?"

Tabby is not sure what he means but suddenly realizes he is talking about a chimney or a sheltered stove. "Yes, of course."

Squishslug's grin grows as he begins to like what he hears. "Would you like a drink? We have wild berry juice."

Tabby graciously accepts and a few moments later, a Man enters the home with two crude wooden cups. The cups placed in front of them are barely able to stand properly. Tabby and Squishslug quickly grab their drinks before they spill.

Tabby bravely asks, "Squishslug, how did you communicate to your Man to bring us drinks?"

"I told him," the leader responds with puzzlement.

"I did not hear you talk or see you give him a signal."

"Oh, now I understand. I asked him with my thoughts."

Tabby's shocked face startles Squishslug slightly.

"Can all Men share their thoughts with each other?"

"Of course. But only if we want to and the others listen."

More ideas fill Tabby's head. *Manbabies ... err ... Men could be extremely powerful with the proper guidance. Squishslug seems very mature, not like the reputation his Men demonstrated in the past.* "How far can you communicate with thought?"

"I believe there is no limit. We have not tested for distance because we are a close community."

"Your unique skill would be quite useful to me. I am willing to give you tools and supplies so you can build a village and craft your own tools to grow food, dismember trees, build fires safely, plow fields, cook, and many other uses. The food and materials you make could be exchanged with other races."

Squishslug enjoys the potential opportunity for his Men to become self-sufficient. "We also want chalk sticks so we can draw, paint so we can cover our mistakes, and motherly love."

Tabby sits motionless. *How can I provide motherly love?* Squishslug enjoys his drink while Tabby thinks hard about his next sentence. "I can bring chalk sticks and paints. I can help you find motherly love, but we would need to work closely together." Tabby cautiously takes a sip of the juice. *This sweet mixture actually tastes good.* "Your Men have many skills and talents, which I would find very useful with the upcoming festival."

"Ohhh! Yes, I love festival. So much fun!" blurts out the childish side of Squishslug.

"I am told it will be a very large festival. I need your help protecting the people and children at the event. The Nymphs will be there, and they could possibly give you the motherly love you need."

Loud cheering can be heard outside. The ground rumbles as hundreds of Men do their ceremonial jumping dance.

"The Men agree to your proposal, DuHero's friend," Squishslug says. "Let us discuss the details."

Tabby realizes he just was negotiating with all the Men in the village under a guise of DuHero's reputation.

Chapter 15
Announcement

F lagrot is confident his preparations are underway to make the festival a success. Using a PhishFone, he contacts festival coordinators from the other kingdoms and gives them the date and location for the festival. He receives definite confirmation of attendance from the Nymphs and the Porcs. During the conversations, he learns of interesting news from both associates. Many more Snobs are expected to attend the festival, but their agenda may differ from normal festive activities.

When the Snob representative speaks with Flagrot, there is caution in his words—no surprise, considering Flagrot also heard from his spies that his head is going to be the centerpiece in an illegal trophy room somewhere in Snob territory soon after the festival. Flagrot had asked Tabby to convince the Porc leadership to attend the festival in full force and bring the proper equipment. Now, Tabby reluctantly complies and adds this task to his already busy schedule.

Flagrot passes most of the news to Refailable. Although the Goon leader is pleased that the Nymphs have abolished their sex discrimination laws, he is frustrated that DuHero is the hero of the Nymph revolution. Refailable tells the Minister of Miscellaneous Flaggotry that he wants to hold a public meeting in the arena.

Later that day, the arena horns blast at predictable intervals to inform all Goons that there will be an event at the arena. Ten blasts of the horn is the start of the countdown. This gives Goons from far distances lots of time to travel to the arena. When the count reaches one long horn blast, the meeting begins. The crowds of Goons talk boisterously and play mob games to pass the time. Refailable walks on to the front right stage and cough-grunts in the dongmike. The rowdy crowd pays no attention to their illustrious leader. The Minister of Miscellaneous Flaggotry walks to Refailable.

"Flaggots!" says Refailable. He waits for silence but of course none will come. "Flaggots!"

The crowd continues to ignore him, knowing their incessant rowdiness will make their leader go crazy. Refailable sighs and pulls out his crossbow from his back pouch. He scratches the head of an arrow on a rough rock pad sitting on his left hip. As the arrow lights into flame, he loads the crossbow and aims at an unsuspecting talking Goon. One headshot later, he repeats the exercise. Normally, his antics only take two or three arrows to quiet the crowd. After eight arrows, the crowd is somewhat focusing their attention to their leader. Refailable can feel his control of Goons fading. The Minister of Miscellaneous Flaggotry raises his arms, and the audience quickly silences. Refailable's mumbled curse words can be heard through the dongmike.

"Flaggots! The festival date has been set. Starting thirty sunsets from now, the celebrations will begin!"

The audience mumbles and cheers a bit, but most are not enthusiastic. Refailable is not surprised at the mediocre reaction. Goons throw their own festivals constantly and having to travel a long distance to enjoy themselves is not appealing.

Once again, I need to stimulate my stupid fat masses. "Goons! This will be the biggest festival ever! I promise all of you there will be something for everyone!" he bellows. He pauses but still there is no enthusiasm. "There will be food!"

"*Food!*" yell some Goons who obviously love to stuff their faces with anything edible, including dirt occasionally.

"There will be drink!"

"*Drink!*" scream more Goons who need drinks to continue their constant stupor to make stupidity.

"There will be war!"

"*War!*" growls the audience, along with bloody screams of roaring zeal.

"There will be women!"

Everyone falls silent. One Goon asks, "Are you serious?"

"Am I serious? Yes! The Nymphs have removed their no-sex laws. They want to be with Goons!"

"*Boobies!*" the entire crowd echoes. Now the Goons are ready for the festival.

The Minister of Miscellaneous Flaggotry leans to Refailable and whispers, "Nymphs want Goons, sir?"

Refailable whispers back, "If I'd said Nymphs wanted men, no Goon would go to the festival."

Chapter 16

Dumbness versus Craziness

Flagrot's voice speaks through the PhishFone. "Hello, DuHero. Good to hear from you. Congratulations on the revolution. You are the most popular Goon in our kingdom."

"Flagrot, I need your help. Juulia has gone insane!" DuHero desperately says to the PhishFone.

"What do you mean?" the PhishFone says back.

"She isn't the same Juulia we know her to be. Is there a curse or chant that makes women crazy?"

"Well, no. The term 'crazy women' is redundant." Flagrot chuckles. "Women and craziness embrace each other closer than love."

"I do not understand," DuHero says.

"There is an old adage from day one of my existence. In relationships, men become dumb, and women become crazy."

"Yes, yes, I understand. Tell me how to fix this."

"I need to know what you did before I can assess the damage."

DuHero collects his thoughts. "We woke up in her hovel, and she was telling me all the problems she needed to solve for that day. She had so much to say, and she sounded troubled. I tried to give her practical solutions and tell her not to worry about it.

Juulia eventually grew frustrated. I tried to gently hug her, but all she did was squeeze me and break my ribs."

"Mmmm. Go on," Flagrot mumbles.

"While I was waiting for my ribs to heal, I came up with a plan to slay a beast that was terrorizing a village just outside of the city. That duty was one of Juulia's responsibilities, and I knew she couldn't do it today. I died three times, but I finally killed the threat and brought the beast's head to Juulia while she was negotiating with her sisters in an outdoor meeting in the city."

"And instead of your receiving a thank-you, she went crazy."

"Yes. Exactly. After what seemed to be an eternity of her screaming at my face, I covered my ears ... err, ear."

"More crazy?"

"Yes. So much more. She tore my trophy ear off her belt, unchanted it, and stabbed it to pieces on their meeting table. I thanked her for returning my ear. That is when she foamed at the mouth and tried to kill me!"

"Where is she now?"

"Unconscious on the ground underneath me. I had no choice." DuHero looks down at the calm face of his fallen love. Members of Juulia's meeting keep their distance, knowing to never interfere in a domestic dispute.

Such a contrast from a few minutes ago. Please relax, Juulia.

"Well, I must commend you for being a man," Flagrot says in a calm, dull tone. "Too bad women do not understand men very well. I believe you broke so many unwritten women laws that I do not know how you can recover."

DuHero is shocked and speechless. Flagrot continues. "Women expect you to read their minds and expect ten times the attention they give you. That beast head was only a small token of affection compared to the numerous blunders you made toward her. She may need to kill you a few times to make her feel better."

"Uhh, all right, if it will help. She is waking up, so I am going to keep my distance so we can negotiate a truce."

"No, wait, DuHero! She—" Flagrot tries to stop him but Juulia interrupts.

"Who is on the PhishFone? Your other pushim mate?" Juulia screams.

"What?" DuHero says.

"Hello, Juulia. This is Flagrot." The fish speaks with Flagrot's voice.

"You! You! You told me to invite that chicken head of a hero to my kingdom!" Juulia says while tears roll down her face.

"Congratulations for removing the anti-sex rule—" Flagrot says and is immediately cut off.

"Aaaaahhh! I hate you men! All of you are conspiring to extinct us and steal our children!"

"Juulia, please—" Flagrot begs.

"You! Dumb-zero! Do we live for each other only to know when the other is dead?"

DuHero and the PhishFone look at one another, contemplating their next step. Both tacitly agree to say or do nothing.

"I am done! All of you can die in a fire for the rest of your existence!" Juulia runs to her saddled bird and mounts the large beast. As she becomes airborne, she screams back, "I am leaving you to have my baby!"

DuHero feels destroyed. He does not know how to react after losing Juulia and, apparently, a potential child. DuHero and Juulia are supposed to travel to the festival together by foot. He decides to slowly walk to the festival, even though the event does not start until many sunsets from now.

"We will talk later, DuHero," the PhishFone says. "There are plenty of fish in the ocean."

DuHero primes his arm and throws the PhishFone deep into the city.

Hunger never rumbles his stomach. He feels no thirst or fatigue; just sunset after sunset, he walks slowly. All around him, life continues. Animals still run, Nymphs hug each other, the sun still moves, night always comes. In his heart, his existence seems to stop. The emptiness eventually turns to anger. *I need an excuse to kill something!*

No excuse is needed as he chops and chops a helpless tree with his sword. The squirrels in the tree do not appreciate his woodcarving skills and chirp loudly at the troubled Goon. DuHero climbs the tree, hunting squirrel. He succeeds in stabbing a bee nest and succumbs to hundreds of stings as he runs, cowardly, from the branch, down the tree, and toward a stream.

DuHero does his moping and violence ceremony day after day. No tree is safe. The only time he feels accomplishment is when he kills an old kid with chanting balls that steals animals from their habitat. DuHero also kills some guy dressed in a silly green suit who had lots of gems and assorted worthless objects in his pouch.

The silly green man's sword and bow is much better that what the Nymphs made for me. The green-suited fellow tries to retrieve his equipment but is always met with an arrow to the face. At the graveyard, DuHero sits on a gravestone and shoots the helpless man in the head each time he re-exists. Once the quiver is empty, DuHero tosses the bow.

"Thank you, green man," DuHero says to the bewildered man, surrounded by dozens of his corpses. DuHero is ready for the festival.

Chapter 17
Festival of Destruction

Thousands of creatures pour into the huge valley near the Great Door and the DNA Chamber. Flagrot is confident no one will discover these hidden treasures. All the creatures cooperate and move toward their designated zones. Flagrot designed the segregation of kingdoms in the exact geographic setup of current kingdom representation. From one side of the valley, Goons are situated at the far left corner; Snobs, upper right corner; Nymphs, lower left; and Porcs, lower right. At the center of the four groups is a very large, painted green circle, where races can interact in peace, similar to a neutral zone. The intention of Flagrot's territorial divide is to allow races to enforce their own laws within their makeshift kingdoms of the festival. The green peace neutral zone is enforced by Flagrot's Manbaby Men, and no kingdom has authority in this area. The green zone also allows minority races and cultures to participate. In previous festivals, without designated boundaries, Goons would go rampant with their shenanigans, and unnecessary fights would erupt, kicking the intended spirit of peace in the backside and laughing at her tears. Now, if Goons go wandering into other territories, they will be killed instantly, unless they have been invited and escorted. The valley can accommodate hundreds of thousands of creatures on the ground. Nymphs construct gigantic perches so their flying creatures can rest and watch the chaos, high above in safety. They close off the ground area around the roosts so no one sees the creature excrement facilities. Goons have constructed elaborate wooden mazes and climbable structures so children can play. Although Goons do help when true charity is needed, their alternative motive is to lure Nymphs to their area for physical intimacy.

The Goon plan seems to be working. Many Goon and Nymph children play near the Goon territory in the green circle, and the happy excitement attracts many smiling Nymphs. Goon children teach Nymph children the chants they learned at Goon school. They are all motivated to practice because they expect to use their skills during the festival. When the children are skilled enough with their chanting, Goons act like a small army and pretend to invade and capture the kids. Kids scream with delight as they frantically try to chant ways to stop the Goons. The Create Water chant is popular and fantastically disorganized. The children wet themselves and some Nymphs more than the silly-acting Goons.

A Goon yells out, "C'mon, kids. We know you can take us down! Try different chants."

The Goons regret that challenge. One Goon has his hair set on fire; many are frozen on the spot, as it rains oatmeal, frogs, sticks, torch lights, and the occasional cat. The ground turns to pudding, and trees sprout and drop huge oranges from their branches. Some use an incomplete Transfer Object chant, and Goons have their arms and heads fly into the festival crowds. Goons, Nymphs, and children are on the ground, laughing so hard. A few Nymphs yell to the kids to stop but cannot stop laughing at the chaos. A Nymph chantress thaws out the Goons and digs out a few who are almost consumed by the rainbow-colored pudding ground. The Goons who are still alive congratulate the kids and walk over to the Nymphs to introduce themselves.

Tabby is also enjoying the festivities; he juggles children and axes at his makeshift blacksmithing and weapons booth. He has brought a huge assortment of gear to the festival and hopes his entertainment will attract customers.

Everyone at the festival enjoys themselves, even though the Snobs barely have a presence. The Porc area of the green zone receives a lot of attention. Goon inventions and Porc chemists made a makeshift show-and-tell area to promote their discoveries and inventions. Porcs are well-known for their mastery at chemicals and fluid concoctions. This year, they've brought lots of supplies and interesting items, and many Goons and Nymphs are excited with the wide selection. The Nymphs huddle around a female Porc vendor to learn about bath soaps, hair wash fluids, body lathering lotions, and sensual perfumes. The Goons experiment with the different ales and hard drinks that made them stupidly happy. The more sensible Goons look at lubricants, explosive fuels, poisons, liquid bombs, and fireworks.

The Goon inventors bring lots of new toys to demonstrate to the crowds. The children love the sillier stuff, like soft hammers that make a gonking noise when striking someone, air boards that allow kids to fly, kick balls with behavior problems (they insult everyone and roll around randomly), and a kiss gun for the girls to drive the boys crazy. The male Porcs are impressed with the advancement of Goon weaponry. Their newest CATapult design is stronger and can launch more cats over a longer distance. The cats also have better armor and weapons, so they can devastate armies with precision attacks against weak spots in a battle line. The thousand-shot pebble cannon is impressive at destroying targets, along with itself. An elongated cannon points at a mountainside. Goons dare each other to become a projectile, and the crowds laugh as a Goon would fly into the mountainside, leaving a blood splotch mark. Eventually, the blood splatters form a large smiling face.

Goons and Porcs chat about partnerships and potential hybrid inventions between the two races. The wise creatures meet in the center of the green circle, exchanging philosophy and debate.

"Anyone who is a man will always want his dong longer than the next guy," a wise man says. The men in the crowd nod in agreement, while some women laugh at the silly notion.

"A bloody nose is a good indication of a successful insult but a bad dodge," a Goon wise man says, with humorous overtones and a broken nose.

"Time is constant. Wasted time is variable. Universal time is infinite. Our time is limited. My time counts for nothing," says a wise man in a drab red loin cloth. At first, the crowd is stunned at the insight, but then applause fills the air as everyone compliments the profound observation.

Nymphs are either with children or studying Goons for potential pushim. Lots of food, drink, music, and entertainment are offered. The party continues late into the night. Flagrot has installed a large dongmike on a tower in the center of the green zone.

He makes an announcement:

Hello, my name is Flagrot. I am the organizer of this festival.
The night is upon us. Please show your consideration and calm your activities so many can sleep.
Tomorrow will be another festive day, so please rest at this time.
Thank you.

As usual, a few Goons do not comply, and they are thrown into a Drunk Shack far from the festival so they can sober up.

As the morning sun lights the valley, the thousands of creatures begin the festivities once again with a morning meal. The Nymphs offer a wonderful, huge meal for Goons and Porcs alike. The massive vats of swamp slime soup and baked bread earn the respect of Porcs, while the poultry, meat, and deep-fried dough makes Goons vomit with overstuffed joy.

Flagrot is impressed with the Manbaby Men who maintain order and discipline throughout the festival. Their thought-communication capability makes it easy for his orders to be delegated to all corners of the festival. The Men enjoy the opportunity to be a useful group at an important event. Flagrot even lets them harass and kill Blantor a few dozen times. Blantor is a Goon deeply hated by Manbaby Men.

When Manbaby Men stayed with Goons, Blantor would use Manbaby Men to do all sorts of slavery work, which would get them killed numerous times. Manbaby Men declared that they would never tolerate Blantor's presence again, so any time a Manbaby Man sees Blantor, they throw him into Porc territory and promptly kill him—he is hated by Men and Porcs alike. Manbaby Men learn how to trophy-chant body parts and decide to use Blantor's head as a catch ball between Men patrolling the green zone.

Goons find the headless Blantor's body. They promptly stuff the body into a cannon and fire him into the mountain wall.

From his central watchtower, Flagrot observes the activities that surround him. He is proud of his achievement to convince the tens of thousands of creatures to attend his festival and for laying the groundwork in securing his future as a shadow power broker. He sympathizes with the ignorant masses at their fake concept of happiness, peace, and the onslaught of chaos he will introduce to the land of Forever in the future.

Flagrot pretends to lecture everyone at the festival, but no one is in range to hear him. "Peace is nothing but a war wrapped in perceived comfort. War is all around us under the guise of ambition, challenges, struggles, needs, and agendas. Goons are at war with their insecurities, boredom, and acceptance. Nymphs are at war with their emotions, instincts of maternity, and acceptance. Snobs are always challenged with cultural acceptance, ego, vanity, pride, and placement within a strict hierarchal structure. Porcs are a mysterious race. Their presence at this festival, with goods made for other races, leads me to believe they seek acceptance among the humans."

Flagrot looks into the far expanse beyond the festival territory with a magnifying eyeball he uses to see far distances. "Tomorrow should be the day when history will be made."

In the far distance, a huge Snob army approaches the festival.

The day continues without too many problems. A few unscheduled fights break out between Goons and Porcs. Some Goons and Nymphs are so desperate to fornicate, they cannot help displaying their intimate affection in front of hundreds of witnesses. Flagrot's Men quickly construct shelters for the amorous, and mini-fight rings so disputes can be resolved. A few young Porcs slap a gooey substance on the backs and bottoms of Goons which, when ignited, propels them forward at high speed. Although Men are amused to see Goons flying, on fire, around the festival, they put a stop to the dangerous pranks.

DuHero receives random kisses from Nymphs as he walks through their festival territory. He loves the attention but his heart is still for Juulia. DuHero makes polite conversation. Six young Nymphs follow him closely as he walks to the Goon festival territory. Refailable sees DuHero's entourage, along with dozens of jealous Goons. As two Nymphs cling to DuHero's arms, he walks toward Refailable, and before he can speak, Refailable says, "Eat a bowl of dongs," and charges off, pushing Goons aside.

The Nymphs and DuHero are confused but their concern quickly passes. DuHero remembers how much he enjoys talking to Nymphs. "Ladies, let us find food and drink. I want each of you to tell me all about yourselves." The six Nymphs become giddy and blush.

At dusk, the Snob army camps on the outskirts of the festival to draw minimal attention. Flagrot sends word to his festival allies to prepare for tomorrow. Approaching his central observation tower is a Snob representative, wearing colorful clothing, decorative jewelry, and a sash to symbolize his authority as a diplomat.

Flagrot waves the diplomat to climb up the central tower. The Men protecting the tower cautiously let him pass. Flagrot extends his hand to help the diplomat reach the top platform, while secretly chanting Transfer Object.

"Greetings. I am Snob diplomat Valdarn for the King Supreme Leader Tenoshin Tabra. King Tabra seeks your urgent audience and requests you follow me to our encampment."

Flagrot stands silent, staring into the eyes of the soft-faced man.

Deception is a common trait among Snobs. Even with diplomats. "I have a PhishFone. Have your king contact me. Ask for Flagrot—but of course, you know that." Flagrot knows his comment is an insult to Snobs, who value face-to-face communication.

"Not possible. Please follow me so we can resolve this matter quickly."

Before Flagrot can refuse the offer, an object tears through the diplomat's clothing and attempts to hit Flagrot in the chest. The object dangles on Flagrot's clothing, barely penetrating the weapon-resistant cloth. The assassin cloaks into invisibility while Flagrot chants Hover Area, followed by Decloak Gas. The chant works as the assassin's cloak is neutralized. Flagrot immediately notices the assassin diplomat has moved behind him, armed with a gleaming cut-throat blade. The Scrunch Genitals chant leaves the assassin keeled over and helpless, hovering above the ground.

"Need to escape," the groaning assassin says as he reaches to his belt. The assassin vanishes.

Flagrot knows only high-level assassins use teleportation devices, but the rare tool is only used to get them to very hard-to-reach places. Teleporting to run away from a fight is normally dishonorable assassin behavior. Flagrot quickly concludes he is in serious danger and leaps off the tower, chanting Rabbit Eagle Speed. The tower explodes as Flagrot crashes into a group of philosophers heavily in debate at a safe distance from the burning tower.

The group recovers, and one member asks with a slight drunken slur, "Do you fear life after death?"

"Only when Snobs grace my rebirth," Flagrot says.

The flaming wreckage of the watchtower draws everyone's attention. Flagrot's Men stay close to Flagrot as he chants hundreds of long wooden sticks and white fluffy treats for the gathering crowd. He grabs a stick, places a treat on the end, and walks to the fire. As the treat roasts, the Men follow his lead. Soon, everyone in the immediate area grabs the sticks and uses the burning structure as a huge campfire for cooking. Flagrot whispers Teleport Person and Speak Silence chants. The assassin diplomat appears, deep in the burning structure. No matter how much the assassin screams, the crowds surrounding the fire are enjoying the blazing event and are unaware of the burning Snob.

Flagrot spends the rest of the evening warning the Goon, Nymph, and Porc leadership of a large potential conflict the next day. Not wanting to cause panic, the leadership inconspicuously prepares contingency plans in case the Snobs plan more festival disruptions.

As morning approaches afternoon, Porc, Goon, and Nymph children are awake, playing as a large group in the green zone. Many tired adults sit nonchalantly enjoying the show of innocent children, free from worry as they play games that make everyone smile. Thousands of creatures soak up the sun, regaining their energy from several days and nights of delight. The sounds of happy children and cooking food are slowly overcome by thunderous rumbles. The Snob army moves into their designated territory at the festival. Many adults turn their attention to the tens of thousands of Snob troops, along with large weapons of war that are dragged behind the hundreds of resource wagons and horses. Snobs are well known for their pageantry and show of strength, but this demonstration is unusual, displaying at the all-purpose festival. The army continues marching, leaving their designated territory and entering the green neutral zone. The children notice the large armies and stop playing. Dozens of children huddle together, frantically exchanging ideas and laughs. They swarm around each other like bees, sharing their sweet enthusiasm with other kids. Soon, hundreds of children are grouped together. After a few minutes, they all stare at the approaching Snob troops.

"Now! Now! Now!" the child ringleaders yell.

All the children run toward the Snob troops. The soldiers show no concern for the children—until chants begin obstructing their progress. Snob soldiers are being soaked, chilled, blown back, and suspended, and some are sunk into rainbow-colored mud. All sorts of chanting mayhem is initiated by the mass of children. Snob archers fall to the ground, dropping their loaded crossbows. The temperature of their weapons changes, and the impact of hitting the ground makes crossbows misfire their payload into the backs of fellow Snobs. They also misfire into the mass of children. Many children die their first time.

Hundreds of arrows spray the children. Only after the screaming starts does the entire valley of creatures notice the butchering of innocence. A young girl with pigtails runs frantically in the direction of a pack of Nymph mothers, crying wildly as a burning arrow dangles from her arm. A Manbaby Man charges in and picks up the little girl, sheltering her from further piercing carnage. As he runs with the child, he sends a message to his Man brothers that the Snobs are attacking children. Six arrows in the back make the Man collapse. The little girl runs to the Nymphs, who are frenzied at seeing this travesty. A few dozen Nymphs try to reach and retrieve the scattered children, but they, too, are cut down by aerial death.

"*Stop you fools!* Do not attack!" the Pink Knight screams with treble pitch at his generals. *The entire festival will turn against us. The fools!*

His orders come too late. Porcs storm the Snob heavy-armor defense. Because Porcs also have children in the chaos, they throw smoke bombs anywhere a child is still alive, hoping the concealment will protect them. Both Porcs and Snobs are well prepared, and a bloody, noisy melee commences.

"Fight now! *Fight!*" cries the Pink Knight.

Porc artillery takes advantage of the chaos and smothers the Snob rear ranks with flammable fluid bombs, sending hundreds of Snobs to their instant death. The Pink Knight orders his light armor infantry to flank the battle lines and destroy the Porc artillery. Taking advantage of the Goon confusion, the Pink Knight orders his artillery cavalry and heavy artillery projectiles to hit the Goon encampment while they are trying to organize. The artillery cavalry, lightly armored men with small flak cannons strapped to the sides of their horses, use their speed to quickly attack weak positions in a battle line and tear up soldiers and lightly protected equipment.

The Snob king does not like what he sees on the battlefield. The Snob army is strategically organized to fight Goons and Nymphs. With Porcs as an adversary, both sides will suffer huge losses of pride and resources.

The Snob cavalry decimates Goons at an alarming rate. Goons, with no weapons against fast flak-firing horses, turn the Goon encampment into a bloodbath. The Pink Knight hopes to catch Flagrot off guard within the Goon territory or the green zone and put the powerful chanter in a graveyard for quick capture. Little does the knight realize that Flagrot is far from danger, hovering high in the air, invisible and watching the destruction.

Charging from a small hill behind the Goon festival border, thousands of bunnies attack Goons from the rear ranks. Some of the bunnies in the attack mob scan every creature they can find, looking for the lost boy-king. Those Goons that survive the first Snob attack are promptly covered in bunnies, gnawing on their flesh. Dedicated carnivorous bunnies can eat a man to death in four minutes.

The Nymph queen Danashia screams out, "Find anything you can use to kill those scum Snobs!"

The Nymphs and Goons pick up any weapons they can find.

They raid the nearest merchant, which happens to be Tabby. Tabby pleads with the Nymphs to stop looting his wares. He knows any pleading to Goons will fall on deaf ears. Small brown bags filled with gold pellets and jewels fly to Tabby as the Nymphs pull weapon after weapon off his display racks. The blacksmith's body became bruised from the bags hurled randomly at high speed toward any part of his body. He feels ecstasy as each welt aches with another impact of a pouch filled with riches.

The Nymphs line up. They wait for the order that will satisfy their motherly bloodlust. From the sky, a large bird, armed with an assortment of strange, sharp metal objects secured to each feather, plants itself in front of the Nymph line. A Nymph, barely clothed and wielding a large banner, runs and jumps onto the bird. She studies the Snob line and then jolts the bird to turn quickly so she can observe the current battle. She turns back to her sisters and begins a strange battle cry.

"*Why?*" she screams.

"Because!" the line of women bellow back.

"*Why?*" she screams again.

"Because!" they ferociously respond. The feminine army is ready.

Flagrot smirks, as he knows the battle call. To men, the unusual battle cry makes no logical sense. To Nymphs, and perhaps all females throughout Forever, the cry represents instant justification for females to accept emotionally based atrocities. Flagrot thinks to himself and smiles. *This period of the battle is going to be extremely bloody and quite entertaining.* Flagrot studies the Nymph battle group and smiles even more. He notices their belts and sashes are filled with assorted trophy-chanted body parts of defeated opponents.

Out in the land, there are numerous entities missing fingers, ears, noses, dongs, and many other extremities that dangle as morbid female jewelry. Someday, they will come for revenge. But not today.

Then the death call comes. "FUGLYMAN EXTINCTUS!" Although Nymphs have dropped their man-hating laws recently, they still have the traditional man-hating ceremonial cries. Many from the Nymph line leap high into the air toward the Snob rear lines. These ladies fly an extensive distance with the equipped assistance of Flight Panties, which give them a dominating advantage for near-ground aerial battles. The battle rages and everything goes well, according to Flagrot's hidden plans.

DuHero and his orgy of six Nymphs step out of the bushes, fixing their clothes, wondering what commotion is making so much noise. They cannot believe their eyes—thousands of people and creatures are having a bloody battle while bunnies eat off Goons' faces.

DuHero's Nymphs want to join the fight, but DuHero tells them to wait and observe. "We need to know who is fighting who, and see where we can make a useful difference," DuHero calmly reassures his new friends. They watch for a few minutes. DuHero is ready. "Ladies, it seems every kingdom is fighting Snobs. Look to the back. Over there." DuHero points to a large group of archers still trying to recover from the children's pudding ground chant. A few Snobs are capable of firing their weapons but most are immobilized and can only throw insults at the battle that rages around them.

"Ladies, follow my lead. We are going to kill those archers," DuHero says, unsheathing his sword. The group of seven sprints toward the helpless archers. Some Snob spearmen see the charging group and try to intercept. All the Nymphs leap high over them, throwing star-like projectiles into the necks and heads of the spearman; DuHero dodges two thrown spears and impales his sword in a stomach and then redirects his blade to slash a throat. Their path is clear, and archers die by the dozens as the seven tear through the Snob rear lines. The remaining Goons see DuHero's carnage and start to run toward the Snob back lines, only to be cut down by the roving Snob artillery cavalry. Nymphs on large hawks swoop down and individually snatch cavalry riders and fling them across the body-riddled ground. The bunnies do well with suppressing Goons from fighting in the real battle. The bunnies even organize an ambush near the graveyard so that many Goons cannot return to the front lines of the battle. The Nymph eagles, who are symbiotically close to their Nymph riders, fulfill a request to send baby eagles to the battle to kill the bunnies. Goon cats, who are at the Porc encampment on loan, start killing bunnies in the Goon festival territory.

The Pink Knight watches as his archery line falls to pieces. He is about to ride to their rescue with his private knights—until a random artillery explosion knocks him off his horse and kills everyone close to the Pink Knight. To his surprise, the Pink Knight survives.

DuHero's Nymphs sustain superficial wounds as they finish killing all the archers. DuHero looks around for their next target. He is about to lead his group to the Snob heavy equipment, but he slips on a pool of blood. His legs fly into the air, and he lands hard on his upper back, with his legs wrapped over his head, his bum sticking in the air, and a broken arrow piercing his neck.

When DuHero re-exists, the graveyard is full of action and drama. Those who died in battle are herded by dozens of Men and Goons. The children who died earlier are huddled together just outside the graveyard, being hugged and held by compassionate Men. DuHero is stunned to see the large, burly Men caring and sympathizing like mothers nursing their distraught toddlers, while at the same time, another Man nails the arm of a Snob to a large wooden board not far from the children. A Goon re-exists next to DuHero. The elated Goon is engulfed in laughter as he enjoys the pleasure of his glorious death.

"Goon, get sword; go back fight!" a Man yells. As the Goon runs to the pile of swords, the Man sees DuHero. "DuHero!"

DuHero smiles and is crushed by the Man hug. "Wha … guuh … what is your name?" DuHero asks.

The Man drops DuHero, brings his left hand to his chest, and proudly proclaims, "I am Blue Butterfly!"

DuHero is proud the Manbabies have started taking identities. A medium-sized man re-exists beside them.

"Blast! This death will certainly hurt my chances for promotion."

Blue Butterfly grabs the man by the face and with a magnificent twist, he lifts and then flings the Snob over his shoulder to an awaiting Manbaby outside the graveyard. The distant Manbaby catches the Snob and proceeds to nail the man's arms and legs to a large wooden board. DuHero squirms a bit, as with each hit of the long nail, the unfortunate Snob lets out a horrendous scream. When the Snob is securely fastened, the Manbaby picks up a section of the board with the Snob and drags him off. Another Manbaby replaces the wooden board and awaits another victim.

"Very smart, Blue Butterfly. You are stopping the Snobs from returning to battle," DuHero says.

Blue Butterfly smiles. DuHero realizes he left his six ladies in the battle. "I wish I could stay, but I need to return to battle. Take care," DuHero says. He runs to the pile of swords. The naked man runs past the children, wielding two swords and no shame.

When DuHero reaches the valley edge, he discovers he is on the other side of the battlefield. Heavily armored Porcs and Snobs smash and slash one another, and neither side is making progress. The Snob heavy artillery is under attack by Nymphs. Goons are still being killed by that large artillery cavalry. Since the closest fight to DuHero is the Snob heavy armor, DuHero charges into the fray, hoping to dodge any killing blows. He knows he cannot go one-on-one with a fully armored Snob, so he runs around the battlefield, slashing unsuspecting Snobs in vital areas of their bodies. This method proves quite effective—he cuts a throat, runs, slices a waist, runs, kicks a Snob down so a Porc can get the kill, and DuHero runs again.

Scouts from the surrounding area of the festival hurry to find their designated leadership. The Snob scout finds his king and reports the urgent news. King Tenoshin Tabra issues the order to immediately retreat. The Goons soon follow, blowing their primary battle horn to the tune of ultimate danger. Nymphs have their own ear-splitting shriek to fall back. The Porcs see that the battle is ending and walk back to their makeshift war camp. They hurry their pace dramatically when the Porc Unigrunt caller bellows a strange growling noise to the battlefield. To DuHero, these loud, unusual sounds fill the valley almost simultaneously. DuHero soon finds himself alone at one edge of the valley, except for the hundreds of bodies at his feet. He does not know the sounds of immediate retreat were issued to all the races. He looks around to see if he recognizes any of the dead. More strange sounds echo across the valley. All the dominant armies merge into one another, including the Snobs. DuHero is dumbfounded at the immediate unity of the kingdoms. As DuHero watches the unusual unity, the armies wave and call out. From DuHero's perspective, he feels like everyone is trying to talk to him. He graciously waves back.

Flagrot smiles and chants Loud Voice. "DuHero!" says Flagrot as his voice echoes across the valley. "Look behind you."

DuHero slowly turns to see a Boortard on the hill in the distance. Familiarity fills his mind; DuHero tries to determine why he knows the stranger. The Boortard reaches into his belt and pulls out a ring. As the Boortard places the ring on his index finger, he grows larger and starts to glow.

"Well, now, this should be fun," DuHero mumbles as he spins his swords with his wrists. He realizes he was seeing the Boortard who killed him in the past. The crowds behind him keep calling to DuHero. He ignores the noise and focuses on battle tactics to kill his killer. DuHero begins to sprint but stops immediately as more Boortards walk over the hill. Thousands more.

Flagrot is well prepared for the Boortard army. After all, he invited them. Goon long-range cannons are armed and aimed in DuHero's direction. The leaders of the four kingdoms hold an impromptu meeting to discuss their next battle. Although there is seething hatred for the Snobs, all kingdoms despise Boortards much more than any hatred they have for one another. Flagrot and other important representatives gather around the leaders. While they debate, DuHero stares at the Boortards. Although the Boortard army looks exactly like the Four Kingdom Ad-hoc Alliance army, the Boortard sporadic stupidity is quite evident. DuHero can see the Boortard tall leader waving his arms, trying to hold back his army, which keeps growing in numbers. Looking back at his Ad-hoc Alliance, DuHero notices the four kingdom leaders do not look like they are ready.

I need to stall the Boortard army. Facing the Boortards, DuHero raises his swords and gyrates his hips. He then simulates his classic 'F' position as he wiggles his hips back and forth. Jamming both swords into the ground and into a dead bunny, he turns, bends the top part of his body down, and spreads his butt cheeks to the Boortards. He turns his body slightly left and then right, to make sure the entire Boortard army has a good view.

If you are at a disadvantage and can't beat the enemy, at least confuse them. A perfect delay tactic.

The Goon and Nymph armies cheer as DuHero continues to insult the Boortards. The Porcs are confused, and the Snobs look away, disgusted at DuHero's oscillating hips.

DuHero notices that the Ad-hoc Alliance huddle breaks and orders are yelled in different directions by various creatures, all along the Ad-hoc Alliance lines. Leaders pass information, war engines move, and large groups of creatures reposition. DuHero is fascinated by the sheer numbers of his new army.

Tens of thousands. The battle will be a spectacular big bloodfest!

DuHero's insides grow warm as he sees the children are encouraged to participate in the battle by supporting the rear lines, like moving resources and preparing chants to defend the heavy equipment. DuHero changes his stance into a one-arm handstand, while waving to the Boortards. His diagonal protrusion falls into his face, so he performs an act which makes both large armies gasp.

At the corner of his eye, DuHero suddenly sees a footprint appear in a pool of blood. He quickly drops down, grabs a dirt-sheathed sword, and slashes the air near the footprint. A thump is heard as a Boortard assassin uncloaks, dead at DuHero's feet. DuHero decapitates the head, trophy-chants, and waves the bloody prize to the Boortards. Again, DuHero makes Goon insult history by forcefully balancing the head on his pride and joy. The Nymphs' attitude toward DuHero changes from amorous admiration to spectacular disgust. Goons who love displays of utter contempt rave at DuHero's antics and cheer with growling hoots. The Boortards have had enough and promptly attack.

"Welp," DuHero gulps. He turns, grabs a second sword, and sprints toward the alliance. Goons laugh as arrows and explosions follow the naked man, while the assassin's head bobbles recklessly around his stomach. DuHero manages to reach the Porc heavy armor line and jumps into the now-organized Ad-hoc Alliance.

"Fire!" Flagrot yells after using his Loud Voice chant. Thousands of paint-filled pouches whiz over DuHero's head. Boortards receive a good dose of Pink Stink and Blueball Rapepaint. Not only are the Boortards now easily identifiable during the battle, many are seriously confused, and their charging battle line turns into chaotic panic. Boortards wearing Pink Stink are chased by Boortards wearing Blueball Rapepaint. The unfortunate Boortards apprehended by someone wearing Blueball Rapepaint receive a surprise sexual experience. Porc artillery fires into the mass of Boortards. Goon artillery continues to paint Boortards, while the Goon bomber cat division runs to the right flank of the Boortards, then sprints into their back lines and spreads out. Hundreds of small explosions light up the Boortard lines, as cats willfully self-destruct.

The graveyard starts to re-exist armorless Boortards. Goons and Manbaby Men promptly decapitate any discovered Boortards and throw their heads to the Nymph chantresses, who promptly turn them into trophies. The bomber cats that appear in the graveyard run back to the alliance rear lines to receive their next payload from the children.

The Boortards pull back to heal, revive their dead, and remove the effects of the paint. Alliance leaders know that Boortards have special powers and an unknown method of rapid communications, so there is no surprise when the Boortard battle lines reform quickly for the next assault.

Flagrot wants a status report from the graveyard. Flagrot turns to Afffriend, the leader of the Manbaby Men during the festival and now impromptu battle.

"Afffriend, ask your brothers in the graveyard how many heads are trophied. A rough guesstimate is fine," Flagrot says.

Manbaby Men have been assigned to almost every battle group to be a communication relay. Their mind-linking capability, now called Manlink, allows instant communication between their brothers.

"Five hundred heads," Afffriend says.

"Tell the leadership we only extincted around 3 percent of the Boortard army," Flagrot says to Afffriend, who then promptly tells all his brothers through the Manlink. The Ad-hoc Alliance leadership knows they need to kill the Boortard chanters, especially those with healing and reviving-the-dead capabilities. They are not worried, as a plan is in place, waiting for the Boortards to make their next move. The delay in fighting helps the cloaked Nymph assassins position themselves on the left and right flanks behind the Boortard army. The Nymphs stand still and wait patiently for their opportunity to strike as Boortards shuffle around, unaware of the invisible threat.

The Boortards charge and focus on the right side of the Ad-hoc Alliance line. The front line, which is filled with Porc heavy armor warriors, shifts to cover the right flank, while Snob heavy armor warriors protect the back and the center. Goon and Porc artillery pour down fiery balls onto the charging mass, while Nymph assassins slaughter the Boortard rear-line chanters. Snob artillery cavalry sprints around the left flank Boortard line, trampling and shooting the weaker Boortards. They keep watch of the Nymphs in case they lose their advantage and are overwhelmed by a sudden retreat.

The graveyard is busy as thousands of Boortards start to re-exist. Goons and Men grow tired and cannot keep chopping heads, so the Nymph chanters ask for legs and feet. Hundreds of Boortards try to run or crawl away. The chanters are nearly exhausted and change their tactics by creating large mud ponds all around the graveyard, except for one narrow passage toward the Ad-Hoc Alliance rear lines. The chanters also add snare vines in the mud to significantly reduce Boortard crawling progress.

The graveyard chanters ask the Manbaby Men to ask the leadership for support. Unfortunately, the Goon and Nymph chanters at the Ad-hoc Alliance artillery in the main battle are told to stay and protect the back lines. The back-line chanters and all the children help to move resources, re-equipping fallen allies and reloading cannons, along with the Nymph bird bombers.

As the Boortards engage the Porc heavy armor warriors, Nymph bird bombers drop pink pipe bombs in the central lines concentrated with Boortard heavy armor warriors. Every section of the Boortard army is being attacked.

Suddenly, a Boortard bird group dives from high in the sky and engages the Nymphs in bird-to-bird combat. Over the battlefield, all aerial combat soon ends, as all birds fall from the sky from Boortard ground artillery, speckling the sky with small, piercing iron pellets.

Flagrot witnesses the elevated massacre and shakes his head. *Boortards have little regard for killing their own to kill an enemy. I would not be surprised if their solution to fighting cancer is to kill the patient. What fools.*

The Ad-hoc Alliance rear-line chanters are alerted to danger by sensations they feel at the core of their souls. Suddenly, a large group of Boortard assassins uncloak and engage the chanters, leaders, and DuHero. Most of the alliance chanters on the main battle rear lines are immediately killed. The chanters' usefulness is moved to the graveyard, as they help their fellow chanters in extincting Boortards. Since Ad-hoc Alliance members and Boortard creatures begin to re-exist at the graveyard in droves, Goons and Men scream at the newly re-existed and tell them to scream back. If they creature screams back, then they know the creature is an alliance member, as Boortards do not audibly speak. Heads and limbs began to pile high around the graveyard, and the mud pits fill fast with struggling Boortards.

The Snob light armor is able to kill the Boortard rear-line assassins. Porc heavy armor warriors are almost wiped out, but the Snob heavy armor warriors fill in the void to re-protect the rear lines. Goon left and right flanks dive into the melee. Goons, who are known for their berserk attitude toward battles, show no fear and promptly run into the center of the Boortard army, trying to target leadership and extremely weak creatures. DuHero joins the Goon suicide surge; his target is the tall, glowing assassin leader. The glowing Boortard sees DuHero approach, along with Boortard comrades failing to protect their leadership. The glowing Boortard cloaks and promptly runs away from the fight. DuHero tries to slash the air, hoping to cut the cowardly Boortard. He instead lets out his frustration on the now-severed spines of Boortard generals.

The Goon artillery is under attack by the Boortard surge of heavy armor warriors. Porc heavy armor warriors struggle to contain the push and soon, their line completely collapses. The Goon cat assassins group, who were kept in reserve for tactical failures such as this, quickly leaps on the Boortards, cutting vital fleshy areas and poisoning victims. The children who are under attack develop enough confidence for a coordinated defense. As Ad-hoc Alliance children randomly chant, one Boortard suddenly finds flaming torches appear in his eye sockets. Another Boortard has his armor heated to a high temperature and is cooked alive. A few Boortards have oatmeal exploding from every orifice, and others receive the crushing weight of a cow dropped from the sky.

All the children work as a unified group, protecting themselves and the back lines.

Much of the Ad-hoc Alliance is destroyed and the fight is close to ending. Nymph assassins continue to slaughter the Boortard rear lines. They prevent the Boortards who escaped the graveyard from retrieving their equipment from the battlefield. The graveyard is surging with Boortards. Suddenly, there are no more Boortards to kill. The Ad-hoc Alliance wins.

No area of the battlefield is untouched by the battle. The littered landscape of bodies, armor, and equipment hides the green zone circle. The festival seems to end, yet the leaders from the four kingdoms meet and exchange pleasantries, as if they were best friends. Their people roar around them, accepting the new relationship and revel in their hard-fought victory.

The Snob king Tenoshin Tabra, donning his gleaming armor, indicating that his role in the previous battle was managerial at best, needs to settle a matter. "My fellow leaders, forgive the Snob kingdom for the inexcusable battle started by my knight's army. Our purpose was to capture the Goon Flagrot for instantly destroying our army earlier in the season. We believe he has a powerful chant or invention that can annihilate armies instantly."

Refailable laughs. The Goon leader, who is covered in dripping cuts and thrashed armor, shakes his head back and forth in disbelief. "Ridiculous! If that fool had such power, he would have used it to kill everyone at the festival, either for humor or a power grab."

"Flagrot has no ability to wield such power. My chantresses would have sensed such potential," the Nymph queen Danashia says. Her battle uniform draws the most attention from the male-dominated crowd.

Refailable cuts in. "He has also been busy with the festival. I know of no invention—not in his possession nor anyone in Forever—that is capable of killing armies instantly."

"We do want not Flagrot harmed. He help us," the Porc leader

Uggy Ug of Four Nine Eight grumbles. The Porc leader towers a head above the other leaders. His black, scarred armor displays an emblem not too dissimilar to the Snob kingdom design.

Quiet tension builds among them.

The queen breaks the silence. "King Tenoshin Tabra. Your armies attacked children. Why should any of us cooperate?"

"My Pink Knight Sir Laffalot of Blazington led me here, and my armies, to hunt Flagrot. I was just an observer until the Boortards joined the battle. We need to resolve this dispute before we can form a peace treaty of any sort," King Tabra says.

Refailable asks, "Do we really want peace?"

"*Peace!*" the Manbaby Men yell in unison. All the armies follow, hailing "Peace!" over and over again.

Refailable does not realize that a Manbaby Man is standing behind him. Refailable mumbles to himself, "I really hate Manbabies."

"Decision by duel!" the Porc leader croaks. "One warrior from each warring army. Winner wins battle. War no more." Each leader looks at another and agrees.

The Snob king turns to the watching masses. "We have decided one-on-one battle to the death between Goons and Snobs. Sir Laffalot of Blazington, step forward," King Tabra says.

The Snobs cheer as their best knight is selected for the duel. The king is happy with his selection. If the knight fails the duel, then the king has the right to strip his knighthood. If the knight wins, the king can take credit for choosing the right knight and receive the glory of good leadership. But in the latter case, he will need to watch the Pink Knight even closer so his throne is not threatened.

Refailable has the same dilemma as King Tabra. Refailable thinks to himself, *Leaders, kings, should never duel in these matches; there is little to gain and too much to lose. It is always best to send in warriors trying to climb the ranks.* Refailable turns to face his fellow Goons. "Who wants to fight the Pink Knight?" Refailable says with reluctance.

Hundreds of "Me's" are given, followed by laughter.

"Give me a name, Flaggots!" Refailable scowls.

"Mr. Me" won the majority. Refailable makes a two-arm gesture, signaling his obscene displeasure with the crowd. Goons chuckle, and Nymphs roll their eyes in displeasure.

A Nymph yells out, "DuHero. Choose DuHero."

Although Nymphs do not have a vote in Goon matters, the outburst rallies Goons to finally give a consistent answer. DuHero's name fills the air.

"Very well. DuHero will represent Goons," Refailable reluctantly proposes to the crowd. "DuHero, get over here!"

Nymphs and Goons cheer. The Snobs and Porcs leadership is surprised a Goon is receiving so much praise from two kingdoms.

DuHero and the Pink Knight approach the four leaders. DuHero receives pats on the back and kisses from both Nymphs and Goons. Snobs politely move to make room for their dueling representative.

The queen speaks. "Gentleman and Goon, battle to the death. Winner wins the battle between Goons and Snobs. A deal has been negotiated between the Goon and Snob leadership, which depends on the results of this battle. Fight like your existence is on the line." The Nymph queen looks at DuHero. "Will someone give this Goon some pants!"

A few dozen undergarments, many female, fly at DuHero. A pair lands on the Porc leader's helmet without his realizing it. "Clear this area!" the queen announces. Hundreds of allies back up as a space opens for the two to fight. A few dead creatures and equipment litter the open ground. No one thinks of removing the potential obstacles. The leaders stay in the opening with the two fighters, and each makes a ceremonious hand sign of "fight well" or "best of luck" to each warrior. When DuHero covers his naked body, the leaders walk away from the challengers and to their designated kingdom armies. Everyone around the circle scrambles to see the competition.

The Pink Knight takes a good look at his competitor and is shocked. "You?"

DuHero carefully raises his sword with his right hand and picks up a dead bunny with his left. He starts spinning the bunny by the tail by twisting his wrist rapidly.

The Pink Knight points his sword at his competitor. "How did you escape?"

The rotating bunny occasionally shoots out blood from its eye sockets, sprinkling red dots everywhere.

"Tell me, traitor! You are not supposed to exist!" the Pink Knight rants.

DuHero grows impatient and rushes the knight. A clank of swords, followed by a slushy gush, is heard as DuHero paints the face and upper armor of the Pink Knight with bunny blood. DuHero backs off, drops the mutilated bunny, and picks up a dead, partially scorched cat. DuHero spins the cat the same way as he spun the bunny.

The Pink Knight continues to talk instead of fight. "Why do you fight for Goons?"

DuHero stops swinging the cat. The Pink Knight has raised DuHero's curiosity. *This Pink Knight knows me?* While they exchange whispered words, bunnies sneak through the crowds, scanning all the creatures, looking for the boy-king. One bunny scans the competitors. His tiny eyes cannot believe what he sees. The bunny gasps, "I found ... I found ... *them?*"

"Who am I?" DuHero demands forcefully as he swings the dead cat, barely hitting the Pink Knight's shoulder.

"Traitor!" the Pink Knight blasts when his power thrust is dodged.

I want answers. "Who ..." DuHero growls as he swings the cat hard enough for its head to explode across the Pink Knight's face. Their swords clank and lock as each fighter grabs his competitor's arm.

"Who am I?" scolds the impatient DuHero.

"Stop pretending to be the fool. Why do you fight for Goons, traitor?" the Pink Knight says while raising his right foot and kicking DuHero in the knee. Their grips release as DuHero pushes away, while dropping the cat.

Lost the cat. No matter. It did not have much life left as an effective weapon.

The Pink Knight's blade swings by DuHero's face. The battle rages until their swords become heavy from fatigue. Their swords lock, and they come face-to-face.

"What is my name?" DuHero demands.

They struggle but neither is moving.

"Don't patronize me, jester," the knight spits out of his bloodied mask.

Jester? Am I a Snob part of the royal court, or is the word just an insult? I NEED TO KNOW! DuHero struggles to catch his breath. "I … I be … became Awared with no memory." He took another deep breath. "Tell me who I am!"

The fight is at a stalemate. The knight is growing tired of the questions. He speaks. "You honestly do not know who you are?"

"No!" DuHero screams with frustration.

Neither side lets up in the struggle. The knight is convinced that DuHero does not understand the range of his past.

"Please," DuHero says. "I know nothing except waking up being a Goon."

The Pink Knight is disgusted with his competitor. He knows he needs to kill this man, or his career as a knight is over. "Drop your guard, and let me kill you," the Pink Knight whispers. Bloody spit runs down through the armor holes near his mouth.

DuHero contemplates his next move. *I need to lose a fight to find my identity. This knight knows nothing of my recent past. I have been a loser for quite a while, and my trail of self-bodies shows my progress.* DuHero nearly loses the grip of his sword as he contemplates that his entire known existence is filled with accomplished failure. *Fine, this fight is not mine but for Goons anyway.* Before DuHero drops his guard, he hears random, joyous, motivational cheers from the crowd.

"DuHero! DuHero!" can be heard from Manbaby Men.

"Our hero, the DuHero!" the ladies from the crowd sing.

"Flaggot! Flaggot!" is choired by Goons.

DuHero's mind races. *I have a new life. Why should an old life haunt my present? I don't know what to do!*

The Pink Knight patiently waits for DuHero's answer. That does not stop him from looking for a potential weakness as they modestly wrestle one another.

I do not want to know. But I need to know something. My curiosity makes me a sadist. My past could hurt me and ... and I might enjoy my wicked history. "I will walk into your sword only after you tell me my *real* name. That is all I want."

The crowd becomes impatient as the two lean on each other for standing support.

"Fine," the Pink Knight reluctantly agrees to the condition. "Your name is—"

An oversized anvil falls from the sky and crushes both competitors.

In the distance, an extremely irate Tabby breathes furiously and screams, "F******K GOONS!"

* * *

The story continues in the book
The Forever Question: Complexperimentation